WARRIORS

Prem Sagar Gupta

<u>About the Book</u>

This book is a collection of four mini novels, titled Roselyn, Honourable Option, Warriors and Damini – The transgender..

"Roselyn" deals with menace of drugs and its dire consequences suffered by Rose. It is a story of her great sacrifice while fighting against drugs to safeguard her family and society at large.

"Honourable Option" deals with social ill of casteism which does not spare even intelligentsia like Bhoop Singh and Archana. Could they manage it?

"Warriors" is a story of five men who set out to free Indian society from widespread corruption. They have an ambitious though unconventional plan to achieve their objective. What was the plan? Did they succeed?

"Damini – The transgender" is a life story of Damini, who suffered for being a transgender for no fault of her.

****

<u>Disclaimer</u>

This is a work of fiction. Names, characters, places, and incidents either are the product of the author's imagination or are used fictitiously. Any resemblance to actual persons, living or dead, business establishments, events, etc. is entirely incidental.

<u>Copyright:</u>

<u>About the Author</u>

Prem Sagar Gupta
B.Sc. Engg. (Mech); I.E.S.
FIE (I); C Eng.; M.Sc. (UK)

The author is a Mechanical Engineer having worked for Indian Railways for more than thirty years in senior positions. He has widely travelled in India and abroad to various western countries. This book is his fourth publication, the earlier three being "Three Daughters", "A Tale of Three Lives" and "Shadows" published in 2020 and 2021.

****

<u>**Dedicated to:**</u>

My Grand Children -

Ayaan, Sanya, Ahaan, Jaskirat, Aditi, Rohan and Tanveer.

Contents

S.No	Title	Page
1.	ROSELYN	7
2.	HONOURABLE OPTION	79
3.	WARRIORS	129
4.	DAMINI - The transgender	182

****

I

ROSELYN

1

Rose

Village: Kharar, Amritsar

Ishwari Devi was born in a family which struggled even to arrange three meals a day for its seven members – father, mother, four daughters and one son. Ishwari Devi was eldest of the five siblings and therefore carried maximum responsibility on her small shoulders to help her mother in household chores as well as to assist her in city homes where her mother worked as a maid to supplement their family income. As a consequence, Ishwari Devi could not study beyond primary school and therefore remained almost an illiterate.

Her father worked as a labourer on daily wage which did not yield enough income to take care of the family needs. Besides, he was also in the habit of drinking liquor frequently which made financial crisis for the family a permanent feature.

To gain some financial help as well as to receive some food items from time to time from city church, family of Ishwari Devi converted to Christianity and she was rechristened as Roselyn.

With passage of years, Roselyn grew to be a twenty years old young and sensuous woman, attractive enough to invite attention of young men in the village. Fearing any untoward incidence involving Roselyn and some village boy, her parents married her off to a twenty five year old boy, named Balwant Singh who lived in Khandera, a neighbouring village.

Balwant Singh belonged to a five member family, father, mother, two sons and a daughter. Balwant Singh was eldest of the three siblings. Other two siblings were Surender, a son, two years younger to Balwant Singh and Sudesh, a daughter, seven years younger to Balwant Singh. While his father worked as a carpenter, his mother regularly stitched clothes for women in their locality as well as for a tailor in the city. They also owned a small house in their village. The financial position of his family was therefore quite comfortable.

Unfortunately for the family, Balwant Singh got into bad company since his early age and could not complete his middle school education. By the time he turned twenty years old, he had tasted drugs. He was a regular in drugs when he got married to Roselyn.

Rama Devi, mother of Balwant Singh was quite hopeful that Balwant Singh will improve and stay away from drugs after his marriage. She had seen Roselyn in a social function and was quite impressed with her beautiful and attractive figure besides her decent manners. She was quite confident that Roselyn will succeed in keeping her son off drugs.

Keeping this in mind, Rama Devi had approached parents of Roselyn with proposal for marriage of Balwant Singh with Roselyn which was promptly accepted by them.

Parents of Roselyn were quite impressed with financial position of Balwant Singh's family and more so by Rama Devi's assurance that she will not demand any dowry whatsoever during the marriage. They did not consider it necessary to verify other aspects like personal conduct and earning ability of Balwant Singh and instead agreed for immediate marriage.

Village: Khandera, Amritsar

After marriage, Balwant and his family members nicknamed Roselyn as Rose. Balwant Singh was quite enamoured by the sensuous figure of his wife and spent most of his time in her company. Rama Devi was quite happy to see his son's attraction towards Rose and her confidence in Rose's ability to take away her son from drugs, grew manifold.

Exactly after ten months on 10th October, 1995, Rose gave birth to a baby girl who was named as Jyoti. Everybody in the family was happy and considered Jyoti as their Lakshmi, the Goddess.

Balwant was quite fascinated by the small baby and spent most of his time with her. For him, Jyoti had become another attraction besides his wife.

With addition of Jyoti in the family, Rose became busier with her daughter and as a result, could not give as much time and attention to Balwant as she used to give earlier. As a result, Balwant had more free time which he started spending with his friends. Gradually, he again started taking drugs in the company of his friends.

For Balwant, there were now only two enjoyments - one to take drugs in the company of his friends when out of his house and another to have sex with his wife when inside the house. He was fast losing attraction for Jyoti and spent lesser time with her. Rose noticed this change but did not know what to do to bring back her husband away from drugs. She discussed this with her mother-in-law but she also had no remedy to suggest.

Rose became pregnant for the second time and gave birth to a baby boy on 25th November, 1996. There was much more happiness and celebration this time in the family when compared to last time when Jyoti was born. Balwant was especially elated and he broke the news to his friends with lot of pride and sense of achievement. That day, he returned home late in the evening, heavily drugged.

In a religious ceremony, the baby boy was named as Gurpreet Singh. Balwant was present throughout the religious ceremony but he was visibly under the influence of drugs. Rama Devi and her husband noticed it and felt pained and distressed. They decided to take some drastic step to rectify the situation.

After few days, Rama Devi had a long chat with Rose and thereafter a partition wall was constructed in the house. Balwant was called and told to stay with his family in the smaller part of the house and to manage his family affairs including finances by himself. One month ration and some money was given for his family as initial help and told to manage himself thereafter.

After few days, Balwant started working as a labourer on daily wage. To begin with, he used to hand over all of his earnings to his wife but shortly afterwards, he started spending a part of his earnings to buy drugs and only the remainder he handed over to his wife.

Rama Devi in consultation with Rose, had partitioned the house as a strategy to make Balwant responsible towards his family and to stay away from drugs. But the results were not encouraging. As a result, Rama Devi had to continue helping Rose with money and food items to survive with her children.

January, 2005

One day, Gurpreet suddenly developed breathing problem. He was experiencing difficulty in breathing. Rose became nervous not knowing what to do to help her son and she called out to her mother-in-law for help. Rama Devi came almost running and took Gurpreet to local doctor who also could not do anything to treat the boy for want of required medical facilities and advised Rama Devi to take him to some hospital in Amritsar.

It took about three hours for Rama Devi and Rose to take Gurpreet to the government hospital in Amritsar. After initial treatment and tests conducted by medical staff in emergency section, doctor advised Rama Devi that Gurpreet had a hole in his heart and that he will require an operation at the earliest.

When enquired about expenses, doctor told Rama Devi that operation will be free but there will be expenses on medicines and other items required for the operation which may amount to about twenty thousand rupees.

Rama Devi became serious and worried on hearing about the amount of money. She had only about ten thousand rupees in total at home as her savings for emergency situations. She decided to take loan of ten thousand rupees from lender in the village.

After reaching home, Rama Devi took out ten thousand rupees from her box and gave to Rose for keeping with her till another ten thousand rupees could be arranged from the lender. Rama Devi wanted the operation at the earliest so that Gurpreet could be treated without any undue delay. Rose kept the money in her box.

After few days, Gurpreet again developed severe breathing problem. Rama Devi took out ten thousand rupees taken by her on loan from the village lender and asked Rose also to take out ten thousand rupees lying with her and to take Gurpreet to the hospital.

But to the astonishment of Rose, she found money missing from her box. Rose did not know how the money went missing. She told her mother-in-law about it. Since Gurpreet appeared to be in serious condition, Rama Devi and Rose did not delay to investigate about the missing money and instead took him to the hospital along with ten thousand rupees.

Gurpreet had become unconscious when they arrived at the hospital. Despite their best efforts, doctors could not save Gurpreet and pronounced him dead even before commencement of operation.

Next day, Gurpreet's dead body was cremated as per family's religious traditions in presence of large gathering of the village people, but Balwant Singh was missing. Despite their best efforts, Rama Devi and Rose had failed to locate him anywhere since previous evening after they had brought the dead body home.

Balwant Singh came home in heavily drugged condition two days after the cremation. The news of death of his son did not make any effect on him and instead he wanted to have sex with his wife. Rose could not control her anger and she gave a hard slap on his face and then wept uncontrollably.

Later when enquired by Rose, Balwant Singh confessed to have stolen ten thousand rupees from her box. His excuse for stealing money was to repay the loan on his head on account of drugs consumed by him.

July 2009

Rose and Rama Devi had lost all hopes for any improvement in Balwant Singh's drug habits. They did not know what to do more to keep him off drugs. Keeping this in view, Rose learnt stitching from her mother-in-law and started assisting her in stitching clothes for the clients. She wanted to be self-reliant as she had lost all hopes from her husband.

Jyoti had become almost fourteen years old teenager girl and had developed a good physique. She looked much older for her age and quite an attractive and beautiful young lady. She was studying in ninth standard in local village school and was very good in her studies. Her teacher rated her as a very intelligent girl and had also advised Rose to pay special attention ,m to her education as she had the potential to do well in her life.

Both Rose and Rama Devi used to encourage Jyoti regularly to sincerely focus on her studies and to make an aim to become a senior officer in her life. They assured her all support including finances.

10th October 2009

It was 14th birthday of Jyoti. She was in a very happy mood since she woke up early in the morning. She was wearing her best dress and was looking lovely and beautiful. Few days back, Rama Devi had promised to buy her a new cycle as a gift on her 14th birthday and therefore, she was eagerly awaiting the same.

Rama Devi and Rose had gone to Amritsar city to deliver stitched clothes to their client tailor as well as to collect payment. Rama Devi remembered her promise to gift her granddaughter a new cycle on her 14th birthday and for this purpose, she had planned to buy a cycle while returning home from Amritsar.

Balwant Singh was at home and was readying to go out to spend time with his friends. Of late, he had stopped working altogether and was totally dependent upon his wife and mother even for his meals. He had wished happy birthday to Jyoti in the morning to her utter surprise. Nonetheless,

Jyoti had felt happy when her father wished her happy birthday.

Balwant Singh was treating Jyoti in a very loving and affectionate way since morning.

While eating breakfast, Balwant Singh told Jyoti, "My darling daughter, today I want to give you a gift of your choice. Will you come with me to the market to select your gift?"

Jyoti was quite surprised but she felt overjoyed. After a long time, she had found her father in such an amicable and pleasant mood.

"Oh yes father. I will certainly come", She replied.

"Then get ready immediately so that we are home before your mother and grandmother return from Amritsar", Balwant Singh told Jyoti.

At 11.00 AM, Balwant Singh and Jyoti left home for the market.

Rama Devi and Rose returned home at about 6.00 PM. Rama Devi was carrying a new cycle for her granddaughter's birthday gift.

Balwant Singh was already home in drugged condition and lying on a cot in the verandah.

"Jyoti! O Jyoti! Come here. I have brought your birthday gift", Rama Devi called her granddaughter.

But there was no response.

Rose went inside the house to look for Jyoti but she did not find her anywhere.

"Have you seen Jyoti? Where has she gone?" she asked Balwant Singh who was lying on a cot nearby in drugged condition and blabbering.

"Yes. I have sold her to my drug supplier. Look here. I have ten thousand rupees. Now I am free from all loans on my head. You take this money", Balwant said and threw some currency notes towards Rose.

"Whaaat? Are you in your senses?" Jyoti shouted at Balwant Singh and grabbed him from his shirt collar in a hysterical manner.

"I have sold her for twenty thousand rupees. Ten thousand in cash and no more loans", Balwant Singh again spoke in broken sentences.

"Oh you scoundrel! You sold my daughter for your drugs. How dare you?" Rose shouted and ran towards the kitchen. Soon she was attacking Balwant Singh repeatedly with a large kitchen knife. Balwant Singh was bleeding profusely but Rose kept attacking him with knife in her hand till Balwant Singh was motionless and dead.

Rama Devi and other people from the neighbourhood arrived at the site soon after hearing shouts of Rose. Someone had informed the police. Soon police personnel also arrived at the site where dead body of Balwant Singh was lying drenched in blood. Rose was standing nearby and staring at her husband's dead body with hatred and contempt without any guilt feelings in her eyes and knife still in her hand.

Rama Devi went up to Rose and patted her as if supporting her action.

Rose cried loudly, embraced her mother-in-law and wept uncontrollably.

"Maa! How shall I get my daughter? He has sold my daughter", Rose lamented.

Rama Devi kept patting Rose. She also appeared to have hatred and feelings of contempt for her dead son.

****

The police inspector went up to Rose and asked her to surrender the knife, which she did without offering any resistance.

"My husband has sold my daughter. Please find her. She must be somewhere near the village. If there is any delay in finding her, I will lose my daughter forever", Rose requested the police inspector with folded hands.

"We shall certainly make our best efforts to trace your daughter. Please come with us to the police station. We shall require details of your daughter from you before we can send our search party to trace her", the police inspector said and signalled a woman constable to take Rose in custody.

The police took Rose to the police station and enquired about details of her daughter as well as about friends of her husband. Rose told him as much as she knew.

Thereafter Rose was lodged in the lock up. The police inspector immediately dispatched a police party in search of Jyoti.

Even after forty eight hours of intensive search, the police could not trace Jyoti. The police inspector had also sent her details to neighbouring police stations but they also did not succeed to trace Jyoti.

The police concluded that Jyoti had been taken away out of Punjab state. The police headquarters in Amritsar took over the case and continued efforts to search Jyoti including liaising with neighbouring state police headquarters. But there was no information which could give any hope for early search of Jyoti.

****

The police produced Rose in the court which remanded her in police custody for a week. Thereafter, a charge sheet was filed against her in the court on account of murdering her husband.

During court proceedings, Rose declined to contest against charges of murder levied by the police against her and instead kept pleading with the judge to trace her daughter.

The court hearings continued for about six months. Taking into consideration the circumstances under which Rose committed the murder, the judge awarded a sentence of imprisonment for ten years. Since she had already spent six months in prison, she was to remain in prison for another nine and half years.

Rose had no remorse for murdering her husband but cried repeatedly in court and requested the judge to help in searching her daughter.

The judge issued directives to the police to make their best efforts to search Jyoti at the earliest but there was no progress till the conclusion of the court case against Rose.

After award of punishment, Rose was lodged in city prison in Amritsar. Everyone among the police had sympathy with Rose but they too were bound by the law.

****

2

Jyoti

Amritsar, 10th October 2009

Time: 10.00 PM

It was a farm house on the outskirts of Amritsar city. The prominent name plate on the side pillar of main gate indicated that it was the residence of Jai Prakash Singh Mindha, popularly known as JP among his followers and friends. He was in his early forties and a very active politician having very close connections with big wigs in political and police circles.

At this time, there were four persons in the farm house including JP besides four gun holding security guards posted at the gate and boundary wall of the bungalow to guard JP and other inmates of the bungalow.

JP was sitting in a sofa in his drawing room. Another person, who was also in his early forties and a close politician friend of JP, was also sitting in the sofa near JP. A little while ago, JP had addressed him by the name Manchanda.

The other two persons, both in their twenties were sitting in chairs facing JP and his friend.

"Sir! We have brought the girl and at present, she is in your inner bedroom. She has been given a sedative and is sleeping. She will wake up after about two hours and then will be fit and fine to serve you in any manner you like", one of the two persons, whose name was Ranjit, said. He was specifically addressing JP.

"Who is this girl? How did you get her? Any complications?" JP enquired.

"Sir! She is the daughter of Balwant Singh, a native of our village and one of our regular customer for drugs. He had accumulated a loan of ten thousand rupees on his head and by paying another ten thousand rupees, we bought her from him. She is hardly fourteen but looks older for her age and very beautiful and sensuous. Her name is Jyoti. She is exactly of your liking", Ranjit said.

"Sir! I have just heard that Balwant Singh has been killed by his wife after learning that he had sold her daughter. Police has already arrested his wife and put behind bars", the other person, whose name was Inder, told JP.

After learning this, there were wrinkles on the forehead of JP. Manchanda also became serious.

'She must have told police about her daughter and police must be searching the girl like mad dogs. We have to be careful", JP addressed Manchanda, who nodded his head in agreement.

"How did you bring the girl here? Did anybody notice?" JP asked Ranjit. He appeared to be quite concerned and disturbed.

"Sir! Nobody noticed us. We brought her here in a mini truck fully loaded with wheat bags. She was completely hidden behind wheat bags. Even though the police checked our truck twice on the way, they could not find her and we were allowed to proceed. From there, we brought the girl straight here", Ranjit explained.

But JP remained concerned and disturbed. He signalled something to Manchanda who nodded his head and left saying, "I will check".

After about fifteen minutes, Manchanda returned and told JP that there was nothing to worry.

"I have checked with police", Manchanda told JP. This made JP relaxed.

"Here are your thirty thousand rupees, twenty thousand for your drug loan and cash given to Balwant Singh and the balance ten thousand as your reward. But make sure that there should be no trace whatsoever leading to this place, otherwise you know what can happen. You must not forget case of Ahluwalia who is still untraceable", JP told Ranjit and Inder. There was a very stern warning in what JP told them.

Both Ranjit and Inder bowed their heads with folded hands.

"Sir! Ahluwalia was a traitor and he suffered what he deserved. We will die but will never be the traitors like Ahluwalia", Ranjit told JP with folded hands. Inder also nodded his head to support what Ranjit said. There were clear signs of panic and fear on their faces.

JP signalled them to go and thereafter they left.

JP rose from his seat and went to an inner room of the farm house. After few minutes, he returned with a bottle of imported whisky, two glasses and some snacks.

"Manchanda! Let us make our night colorful", JP said. He then opened the bottle, poured whisky in two glasses and gave one glass to Manchanda.

"Cheers for the young girl Jyoti. To her health and our enjoyment. Let her be the light for our beautiful night", JP proposed the toast and Manchanda reciprocated.

They kept drinking for next more than one hour and then JP left for his bedroom where Jyoti was lying on his bed.

That night, JP and Manchanda took turns and raped Jyoti repeatedly. Initially Jyoti was not aware of what was happening to her but after she became fully conscious, she resisted them fiercely but she proved to be too weak and helpless before the might of two demons.

Jyoti was kept in the farm house for next ten days, fully guarded leaving no chance for her to escape. JP had decided to wait till police had exhausted all their efforts to search Jyoti and situation became normal before transferring Jyoti to her final destination. The concerned people had already been directed to come and take custody of Jyoti.

During this period, a nurse used to stay with Jyoti to feed her and keep her sedated.

****

21st October, 2009

A car with Delhi number plate was moving on Ambala – Delhi highway. The passengers of the car included a young male driver in jean and a branded T-shirt, one well-dressed middle aged man in the front passenger seat and two female passengers in the rear passenger seats. One of the female passenger was a beautiful and attractive woman in her thirties, dressed in a heavily embroidered Punjabi suit with a heavy gold chain around her neck and ear rings. The other female passenger was Jyoti, dressed in blue jean and matching T-shirt, sedated and camouflaged as unwell. She was lying with her head in the lap of the other lady passenger. They were traveling to Agra as their destination.

The car was stopped at three places enroute for police checks but every time they were allowed to go ahead after the man in the front passenger seat told the police that they were a family traveling to Agra and their daughter was unwell.

At night, the car stopped before a building in Agra and Jyoti was taken inside the building.

Next day, a meeting was held in one of the rooms in the building, during which, the man and woman who had escorted Jyoti from Amritsar to Agra were present besides an elderly lady who was in her fifties and heavily made up.

"I will pay you one lakh rupees in cash for the girl and that is the final offer", the elderly lady told the other two who were in fact husband and wife in the business of trafficking young girls.

"Also note that whatever you have told me about the girl, must be correct and there should not be any wrong information whatsoever, especially about her educational background and the fact that she belongs to a poor family", the elderly lady added.

The couple nodded their heads to reassure the elderly lady and agreed for one lakh rupees. The elderly lady paid them the money and thereafter the couple left leaving behind Jyoti in the custody of the elderly lady.

The elderly lady was owner of a brothel in Agra and her name was Kusum Bai. She was having about thirty girls of different ages in her brothel, who entertained the customers with sex, dance and as escorts with rich clients.

Kusum Bai's brothel was quite famous in Agra and neighbouring areas for its high standard of services without fear of law enforcement agencies. Kusum Bai used to pay hefty monthly fees to law enforcement officials to secure their protection for her girls and the clients. For this purpose, she also used to charge very high price from her clients which they paid willingly.

Kusum Bai also took lot of care of her girls in the brothel, both financially and medically to win their loyalty and continued stay in the brothel without creating any scandalous situation.

Kusum Bai used to purchase girls from human traffickers and supply some of them further to brothels in Mumbai for a higher price. This also added to her income in a big way. She had decided to sell Jyoti too to some brothel in Mumbai and hoped for a handsome profit.

Agra, 22nd October, 2009

Kusum Bai was speaking to someone in Mumbai on phone.

"Munna Bai! The girl has celebrated her 14th birthday only a few days back. She is quite plum and has an attractive and sensuous figure. She also has been a very intelligent student at her place. Her name is Jyoti. I think that she will be very useful for your business in long run", Kusum Bai told Munna Bai.

"I have paid a good amount of money for the girl. I will charge two lakh rupees from you. This is the minimum and final price. You will have to make your own arrangements to take the girl to your place in Mumbai as in the past", Kusum Bai told Munna Bai in response to something Munna Bai said from other end of the phone line.

"OK. So deal is done. Make arrangements to take the girl anytime, preferably within a day or two", Kusum Bai told Munna Bai and disconnected the phone call.

Kusum Bai seemed to be quite happy with the deal which she had just finalized with Munna Bai in Mumbai.

"The deal will make me richer by one lakh rupees", Kusum Bai thought and smiled to herself.

She then called her assistant and instructed her to keep Jyoti in guest room and to look after her well.

"Make sure that she eats well. Dress her well too", she instructed her assistant.

"Yes Madam", the assistant replied and then left.

Kusum Bai was confident that Jyoti will not be able to escape from the building, there being tight security in position all around the building.

24th October 2009

A team of three people, two male and one woman, escorted Jyoti in a car from Agra to

New Delhi railway station. The elder male person was about forty years old and the younger one was about twenty eight. The woman was of about thirty five years age. All three were well dressed and appeared to be educated too. They had been deputed by Munna Bai to take custody of Jyoti and to bring her to Mumbai.

Before leaving Kusum Bai's brothel, Jyoti was warned and instructed not to create any untoward situation by attempting to flee while on the way to Mumbai. To make their warning more effective, the elder person also showed her a pistol and warned that they will not hesitate even for a second to shoot and kill her if she made any attempt to make noise or to flee from their custody at any time. Jyoti was panicked by the sight of pistol and warning tone of elder person and she was left with no courage to even think of an escape from their custody.

Taking no risk whatsoever, they also sedated Jyoti before leaving for New Delhi railway station.

At New Delhi railway station, they boarded Rajdhani Express train and were seated in a four berther coupe of AC First Class coach. Jyoti was made to sleep on upper berth away from the sight of even the Ticket Checker.

Next day morning, train reached Mumbai Central railway station. Two persons had come to receive them at the railway station. They had also brought a wheel chair for Jyoti who was sedated before reaching Mumbai.

Mumbai, 25th October 2009

Munna Bai, though in her early fifties, was a smart and beautiful woman. Her manners and self-confidence indicated that she was from a decent family and well educated but had experienced lot of difficult times during her past.

She was sitting in a sofa in a well-furnished room inside her brothel. The brothel building was known as "Pushap House" written in a prominent style on the outer wall of the brothel. Jyoti was sitting in a chair facing Munna Bai.

Jyoti seemed to be completely normal, there being no trace of any sedation or tiredness. She was wearing a jean and matching tee and looking quite fresh and smart as if she had slept well. She had missed her lunch but had compensated by early dinner.

Munna Bai looked at Jyoti for some long moments and then started the conversation.

"Jyoti! I have been told that you were an intelligent student in your school. So I will tell you about myself and my profession. Listen carefully and try to understand what I say. You will have to make your own decision for your future", Munna Bai said while looking at Jyoti.

Jyoti just nodded her head while looking at Munna Bai.

"My name is Munna Bai but you can call be Aunty. I am the owner of this building which is a brothel to outside people. I have about fifty girls working here for me", Munna Bai said and waited for few moments before continuing.

Jyoti was listening attentively.

"My girls work as sex workers, dancers, escorts and drug traffickers. They pick up their trade on their own free will and nobody forces them to practice a particular trade against their will", Munna Bai said. She took a sip from glass of water kept near her and continued again.

"But they cannot leave me and my brothel because I brought them here by paying a hefty price. They work and earn money for me. In turn, I look after them and protect them against law enforcement agencies. I also create a fund for them to secure their future life. If any one of them finds a suitable match and wishes to marry, I facilitate the same and allow her to leave me and my brothel to settle along with her husband", Munna Bai said and continued.

"Jyoti! Since you are only fourteen years old, you cannot join sex trade till you are eighteen", Munna Bai told Jyoti.

Suddenly Munna Bai asked Jyoti, "Are you virgin? Did you have sex with any man?"

"I was raped", Jyoti told her in a painful voice, with her head lowered.

"Who did it?" Munna Bai asked in a very cold tone. One could sense her anger.

"Do you know the culprits and their place of residence?" Munna Bai further asked.

Jyoti told her about JP and Manchanda and also everything about the whole incidence including killing of her father by her mother.

"Do you want to take revenge against your rapists? I will help you", Munna Bai asked.

"How can I? They are very powerful and rich", Jyoti replied.

"I will help you. For this you will have to work hard. Are you ready?" Munna Bai asked.

"Yes Madam. I will even sacrifice my life to take revenge against them", Jyoti said. She looked determined and much older than her real age. There were signs of raging fire in her eyes.

"Firstly you will have to study and complete your graduation. Thereafter, I will train and deploy you in escorts and drugs business which will give you money and power through connections with big wigs. I will bear all expenses for your training", Munna Bai said.

"But you will have to keep focused on your one point agenda – to take revenge against your rapists, without wavering and deviating from the path I will chalk out for you", Munna Bai added.

"I assure you Madam", Jyoti said.

"Call me Aunty", Munna Bai told her. She took Jyoti in her arms and patted her for long time. Jyoti could not see tears in the eyes of her Munna Aunty.

"Take rest for three days and thereafter I will arrange for your admission in a nearby school. You will stay with me and now onwards, do not worry about anything. Focus only on your studies", Munna Bai told Jyoti.

At night, while Jyoti was sleeping, Munna Bai was wide awake and thinking about her own past years.

Munna Bai was born in a well to do family in Lucknow. Her childhood name was Hema. Her father was a gazetted officer in the service of

Uttar Pradesh government and mother was a teacher in a high school. She and her younger brother were the only two children in the family.

Her parents were very keen to provide higher education to their children and for this purpose, both Hema and her brother were sent to convent school for high school education. Hema was quite intelligent and good in her studies. She was also a good singer and participated frequently in music competitions.

After completion of her school education, she took admission in a reputed college and opted for science subjects. After three years, she passed her graduation examination with very high merit, securing 10th position in the university.

It was afternoon of 11th July 1977. She was returning home after celebrating her success in graduation examination with her close friends. On the way, a group of four persons abducted her in a car and took to some unknown place and raped her. Thereafter, they dropped her near Lucknow railway station.

She was severely bruised and shocked. She could not comprehend why and how this had happened to her. She did not have courage to go home and meet her parents. She took a train ticket and arrived Mumbai. Some stranger at Mumbai railway station brought her to "Pushap House" where she met Hira Bai, the owner at that time. Hira Bai heard her with full sympathies and offered a place to live. Hira Bai was very particular that no girl should be forced to practice sex against her wishes.

Gradually, Hema settled in the brothel and with her intelligence, she won the confidence of Hira Bai in management of brothel affairs. In a short time, Hira Bai had started treating Hema as her foster daughter. After death of Hira Bai, Hema became the owner of the brothel as per the will left by Hira Bai. By this time, Hema was rechristened as Munna Bai, the owner of "Pushap House".

Since her abduction and rape in Lucknow, Hema had developed hatred and deep rooted anger for rapists and as Munna Bai, had decided to help all such girls whosoever suffered rape. After hearing Jyoti, she had decided to help her to take revenge against her rapists which she could not do in her own case.

Thinking all about her past and about plight of Jyoti, she slept off.

29th October 2009

Munna Bai made arrangements to admit Jyoti in 10th Class in a nearby school. Thereafter, Jyoti lived under the close care of Munna Bai. She was fully focused on her studies as advised by Munna Bai. She was intelligent and soon she became popular among her teachers and classmates. Whenever, Jyoti brought home her school reports, Munna Bai felt very happy to see "Excellent" grading in the report book. She used to regularly encourage Jyoti to do well in her studies and aim for higher education. Munna Bai saw in Jyoti an image of herself.

20th July 2015

Jyoti completed her college education and passed her graduation examination with high merit, securing first position in her college. Munna Bai was so happy with the success of Jyoti that she ordered a special celebration in

"Pushap House". All inmates of "Pushap House" joined the celebrations and congratulated Jyoti for her success.

Next day, Munna Bai had about an hour long chat with Jyoti to chalk out future course of action for her. She advised Jyoti to function as an escort and also learn the intricacies of drug trade. Munna Bai was already practicing these trades besides sex and dance trades. She had chosen escorts trade because this did not involve sleeping around with men for money. In her opinion, both escorts and drug trades will bring Jyoti in contact with big wigs and help to develop useful connections which will help to take on JP and Manchanda for revenge.

Munna Bai deputed one of her trusted and experienced associate to train Jyoti and make her familiar with escorts and drug trades. She decided three months training to Jyoti for the two trades.

7th November 2015

It was the first assignment for Jyoti as an escort after completion of her training. She was to escort a big businessman who wanted a smart, intelligent and educated secretary to accompany him for business meetings in Mumbai, Delhi and Chennai. The assignment was for fifteen days and Jyoti was to receive thirty thousand rupees as emoluments besides all expenses to be borne by the businessman.

The businessman was a thirty five year old young man, named Sumesh, who owned a chain of businesses inherited from his father. He introduced Jyoti as his personal secretary to his clients during the meetings.

Sumesh had booked separate hotel rooms for Jyoti and himself for the entire trip duration. But on third day in Delhi, he asked Jyoti to share his bed during the night after the business meeting was over.

"Mr. Sumesh, You have engaged me as an escort to accompany you as your secretary for the business trip. Be aware that I am not a prostitute to sleep with you. For future, don't ever dare to ask me for such filthy services lest ------", Jyoti told him. Her face was radiating fire.

"Oh, I am sorry", Sumesh could utter this much only, embarrassment writ large on his face. Thereafter, he restricted himself to work only till the end of trip.

But Jyoti remained unhappy and tense, anger occupying her mind throughout the trip. She had started hating to work as an escort.

On her return to "Pushap House", she told everything to Munna Bai including her dislike and hate for escort's job.

"Jyoti! There are both good and bad people in our society and we have to live with them. We should have the ability to differentiate between the two and strength to fight against bad people since problems can't be solved by running away from them. You did well by giving a rebuff to that idiot Sumesh and I can assure you that he will not dare again to act like that even with any other girl", Munna Bai counseled Jyoti.

Jyoti continued to perform as an escort for about three months before Munna Bai placed her in drugs trade.

April 2016

Jyoti had been working in drug trade since about two months. During this period, she had dealt with both customers and drug suppliers. There was a team of about ten people who were called couriers and their job was to carry drugs to the customers.

Jyoti was quite surprised to notice that their drug customers included both men and women who belonged to so called high society such as film industry, big businesses, politicians and senior government officers etc. Munna Bai had laid down a rule to deal in only superior quality and costly drugs and not to deal with ordinary customers. Dealing with high society customers was considered to be safer since police did not raid them or interfere with them in normal course.

Jyoti had also made plan to shortly visit Mexico which was one of their few sources of drug supplies of very superior quality. The purpose of her visit to Mexico was to identify some more drug suppliers as well as to explore some more superior quality drugs for rich customers.

Jyoti was quite fascinated by the drug trade since she was regularly getting opportunities to come in contact with famous and powerful people. She had not forgotten that her ultimate ambition was to take revenge against JP and Manchanda in Amritsar and these high level contacts could be useful in times of difficulty.

June 2016

Keeping in view interest shown by Jyoti in drug trade, Munna Bai deployed her as Deputy Head in drug trade organization, she herself being the Head. She wanted Jyoti to gain enough experience in drug trade before deploying her as its independent Head.

So far, Munna Bai had been trading drugs only in Mumbai, but Jyoti drew an action plan to set up drug trade in Delhi too. Munna Bai gave her consent and thereafter Jyoti started recruiting agents for Delhi territory. Within next six months, she started trading drugs in Delhi. Munna Bai was happy with additional income source and she was also greatly impressed by the organizing capability demonstrated by Jyoti.

In January, 2017, Munna Bai promoted Jyoti to the position of Head of drug trade organization in Delhi as well as Mumbai.

Next destinations for Jyoti to set up drug trade were Chennai and Hyderabad besides famous colleges and Universities in Mumbai and Delhi. Looking at the speed at which Jyoti was progressing, Munna Bai once remarked that at this speed, she may succeed to spread her drug trade all over India within few years.

Munna Bai however was not in favour of expanding drug trade among students in colleges and universities. She wanted to restrict drug trade only to VIPs, celebrities and rich people. Jyoti promised her to respect her wishes and restricted drug trade only to senior members of the faculty in colleges and universities.

****

September 2018

It was Sunday. Munna Bai called Jyoti to her room and had a long chat about arrangements to take revenge against JP and Manchanda in Amritsar.

Munna Bai had been gathering information about them from time to time through her trusted men and latest information was that they were continuing in Amritsar and had not improved at all. They were still involved in raping young girls belonging to poor families and thereafter selling them to people in different cities.

After a long chat of about one hour, Munna Bai and Jyoti chalked out a plan to hit both JP and Manchanda in Amritsar. Execution of plan was kept by Munna Bai in her own hands as she did not want Jyoti to be involved in it lest law enforcing agencies find any trace linking to her in any way later.

After few days, Munna Bai hired four hit men to execute her plan to punish JP and Manchanda in Amritsar. Munna Bai gave them detailed instructions as to when and how to execute the plan.

October 2018

Newspapers of 8th October 2018 in Punjab carried headlines about some people firing at JP and Manchanda in JP's farm house located on the outskirts of Amritsar. News read as follow:

"During late evening of 7th October 2018, some unidentified persons entered Jai Prakash Singh Mindha alias JP's farm house located on the out skirts of Amritsar and fired at JP and his associate Manchanda with automatic weapons. Police soon arrived at the site of crime but the assailants had fled away by that time.

Both JP and Manchanda were fired at their shoulder and knee joints as well as at their private male organs from close range. Both were found drunk and unconscious by the police on arrival at the crime site and they were immediately rushed to a nearby private hospital where they are said to be out of danger.

Doctors say that they may become permanently handicapped with their legs and arms not functioning. Doctors also added that bullet injuries at their private parts may also make them sexually incapable permanently.

Police also recovered two young girls, heavily sedated and gang raped, from JP's master bedroom. Police is trying to identify the girls and their parents so that the girls can be returned to their parents.

Police suspect that pattern of firing at JP and his associate Manchanda indicates that some one has committed this crime not to kill them but to specifically make them handicapped and sexually impotent to take a sort of revenge against them

A special police team including detectives has been formed to investigate the crime and all its associated details.

Some undisclosed sources have revealed that JP and Manchanda were involved in drugs, sex crimes and trafficking of young girls but police has declined to make any comment on this aspect at this stage".

Munna Bai was listening to someone on phone. Her face indicated that she had received some news of her liking which made her smiling and happy.

After the phone call was over, Munna Bai called Jyoti to her room and said, "Congratulations darling. JP and Manchanda have been punished and your revenge has been completed".

Thereafter she gave all details of the revenge action to Jyoti who also felt happy and satisfied. Faces of both Munna Bai and Jyoti indicated their peaceful minds as if they had got rid of some heavy weight lying on their minds.

****

3

Roselyn

Amritsar, 10th May 2010

Roselyn was lodged in female section of main jail in Amritsar. Her cell had three other women inmates, Prakash Kaur, Raman Kumari and Surjito, all undergoing punishments of imprisonment for 10 -14 years for committing murders. All three were in the age group of thirty to forty years and appeared to be humble and well behaved. Soon Roselyn became friends with them. After Roselyn narrated her crime details, all the three became sympathetic to her, especially for her daughter.

Surjito's crime story was quite similar to that of Roselyn. She had also lost her teenaged daughter due to drug habits of her husband and elder son.

"I have come to know that there is a gang in Amritsar which deals in drugs, sex crimes and trafficking of young girls", Surjito told Roselyn.

"Why police does not catch hold of these gang people?" Roselyn asked.

"I have heard that these gang people enjoy very strong support of highly influential politicians of Amritsar", Surjito replied.

"How can I find my daughter? Roselyn asked.

"Only these politicians can help, especially Jai Prakash Singh Mindha alias JP. He is very influential but also very notorious", Surjito replied.

Roselyn absorbed the name deep in to her memory and decided to contact him to locate

Jyoti after completion of her punishment. She was determined to find her daughter,

****

Every inmate of the jail was required to adopt one trade to learn and practice for eight hours a day during imprisonment. Since Roselyn knew stitching, she opted for it as her trade.

Since Roselyn was quite good in stitching, the jail warden deputed her to train other jail inmates in stitching trade for four hours a day and for the remaining four hours, she used to stitch clothes on her own.

The jail authorities used to organize an exhibition every six to twelve months to exhibit works of jail inmates and for their sale. The money so earned used to be spent for the welfare of jail inmates and to organize other work activities.

January 2011

Roselyn had become very popular among jail inmates due to her being a trainer as well as because of her helping and friendly nature. Every jail inmate had her own story for landing in jail and Roselyn always connected herself to them to share their sorrow.

She was popular even with the jail authorities who liked her for her cooperation and disciplined conduct within jail premises.

She requested the jail authorities many times to help in locating her daughter but they had their own limitations. One information which she got repeatedly from many people was that Jai Prakash Singh Mindha alias JP could help her to locate her daughter. She had decided to contact JP as soon as she gets out of jail.

January 2013

For Roselyn, days passed easily in the company of jail inmates and jail authorities, but nights were difficult. She used to be awake till late nights, remembering her daughter.

"Where will be my daughter? In what condition will she be? Is she comfortable?" she used to keep thinking.

Surender, her brother-in-law and Sudesh, her sister-in-law, used to visit Roselyn at regular intervals. They also could not trace Jyoti in spite of their best efforts. They tried to contact JP as advised by Roselyn but did not succeed.

Rama Devi, her mother-in-law, died in December 2012 after prolonged illness, as informed by Surender and Sudesh.

"She was my best support", Roselyn thought and kept crying and sobbing for a long time after Surender and Sudesh had left the meeting area in the jail premises.

9th October 2018

Roselyn was released from jail after undergoing imprisonment for nine years. Her punishment of ten years imprisonment was reduced by one year due to her good conduct and disciplined stay in jail. She was also paid twenty thousand rupees as her earnings in jail for her labour during jail term.

After release from jail, she went to her in-law's house where Surender lived with his family – wife and two children, an eighteen year old son and fifteen year old daughter.

Memories of her mother-in-law, son and daughter filled Roselyn with emotions and she cried uncontrollably for a long time.

"I had killed my husband in this house. Even after that, I could not get back my daughter", she thought and kept sobbing till Surender came and comforted her.

Roselyn firmed up her resolve to trace and get back her daughter.

"Finding my daughter will be my only aim in life now onwards and first person I will contact is JP", she told herself.

While eating dinner, Surender told Roselyn, "Bhabhi! I have learnt that JP and his colleague Manchanda have been fired at and wounded seriously by some unknown assailants day before yesterday. Police is trying to apprehend the assailants".

Roselyn was shocked to hear this news. JP was the only hope for her to trace Jyoti.

Where is JP now? How can I meet him?" Roselyn enquired.

"He is in the hospital under strict watch of the police. Nobody can meet him without permission of the police", Surender replied.

10th October 2018

At about 09.00AM, Roselyn along with Surender left home and reached the hospital where JP was hospitalized. There were about ten policemen with guns in their hands, guarding the entrance to the hospital as well as the room in which JP and Manchanda were under medical treatment.

Roselyn went to one policeman who seemed to be the senior most among the policemen guarding the hospital entrance and requested for permission to meet JP.

"Why do you want to meet JP?" the policeman asked Roselyn.

"I lost my daughter nine years back. He will be able to help me to trace my daughter. Please permit me to meet him", Roselyn requested him.

The policeman just smiled and told Roselyn to go away as nobody is allowed to meet JP.

Roselyn requested the policeman repeatedly but to no avail.

A man in his mid-thirties was standing nearby and listening to the repeated requests by Roselyn. When Roselyn was leaving the hospital after getting disappointed and frustrated with the police official, the man joined her after some distance and enquired, "Why do you want to meet JP?

"My husband sold my teenaged daughter to some people nine years back and I am told that JP can help me to trace my daughter", Roselyn replied.

"What was name of your husband and daughter?" the man enquired.

"My husband's name was Balwant Singh and daughter's name was Jyoti", Roselyn replied.

"You can try to locate your daughter at Kusum Bai's brothel in Agra", the man said and hurriedly walked away.

Soon another person in his thirties joined the man and asked,

"Ranjit! Why this foolishness? Why did you talk to the woman and told about the girl. This can put us in serious trouble with the police", the person, who was Inder, asked Ranjit. Ranjit and Inder had brought Jyoti to JP in his farmhouse.

"I momentarily felt pity and sympathy for the woman and told her about her daughter. That was my mistake", Ranjit told Inder.

"Let us quickly get away from here", Ranjit said and almost dragged Inder hurriedly along with him.

"I will have to go to Agra", Roselyn told Surender.

"How can we be sure about what that man has told us?" Surender asked her.

"You are right. He might not have given us correct information but I have my sixth sense telling me to believe him", Roselyn replied.

Next day, Roselyn left Amritsar for Agra by train. Surender could not accompany her as he could not leave his work and Roselyn was in no mood to delay her journey to Agra.

12th October 2018

Roselyn arrived Agra early in the morning and took a three wheeler for Kusum Bai's brothel. The three wheeler driver was quite surprised to see Roselyn asking for Kusum Bai's brothel. He knew the brothel but was not able to comprehend what work Roselyn will have at the brothel.

Roselyn was at the brothel in about half an hour and straight went up the stairs of the brothel without hesitating even for a second. She wanted to meet her daughter without any delay.

There was a guard at the entrance upstairs. When enquired, Roselyn told him that she wants to meet Jyoti and Kusum Bai.

The guard asked her to wait and went inside to inform Kusum Bai. After his return, he asked Roselyn to sit and wait inside the room. Roselyn occupied a chair and waited impatiently to meet her daughter.

After few minutes, Kusum Bai came in the room and occupied a sofa seat facing Roselyn.

"Who are you and what can I do for you?" Kusum Bai asked Roselyn.

"I am Roselyn – mother of Jyoti who came to your brothel nine years ago. I have come to meet her and to take her back", Roselyn replied.

"Jyoti! Which Jyoti? I do not remember. I have no girl with me by the name of Jyoti. I get so many girls here but there is no one by the name of Jyoti", Kusum Bai said and started to rise.

"Please try to remember. I beg of you. Jyoti, a fourteen years old girl, was brought to you nine years ago from Amritsar", Roselyn requested Kusum Bai with folded hands and tears in her eyes.

"Oh from Amritsar. I do remember her now. She is not here. She had gone to Mumbai after two days of stay here. You may find her at Munna Bai's brothel in Mumbai", she said and gave her the address of Munna Bai's brothel.

Roselyn thanked her and came out of the brothel.

She immediately went to railway station and fortunately for her, a train for Mumbai arrived at the station after about one hour. She boarded the train and after about five minutes, it left for Mumbai.

Roselyn was now confident to meet her daughter in Mumbai. She was however apprehensive to think in what condition her daughter will be? She murmured her prayers and looked forward to meet Jyoti in Mumbai.

13ᵗʰ October 2018

Train arrived at Mumbai Central railway station at about noon time. Roselyn hurriedly came out of the railway station and took a taxi for Munna Bai's brothel. The taxi driver was quite surprised and had a long look at Roselyn but could not make out anything. It was first time for him that a lady had asked him to take her to a brothel.

Roselyn was at Munna Bai's brothel in about half an hour. After paying the driver, she went up the stairs of the brothel. She met a woman at the main door.

"What do you want", the woman asked Roselyn.

"I want to meet my daughter Jyoti and Munna Bai", Roselyn replied.

The woman looked at Roselyn for long moments and then asked her to take a seat and wait.

Roselyn sat in a chair and waited impatiently for her daughter.

After few minutes, Munna Bai entered the room and looked at Roselyn.

"May I know who are you and what do you want?" Munna Bai asked.

"I am Roselyn from Amritsar. I am mother of Jyoti and have come here to meet her and to take her back with me", Roselyn replied.

"Your daughter has completed her graduation and she is now the head of my business organization. I will call her and you can meet and discuss with her about her future course of action", Munna Bai said and signalled a woman to call Jyoti.

In few minutes, Jyoti entered the room and looked at Roselyn for about a minute before she ran towards her and took her in her arms.

Both Roselyn and Jyoti remained glued to each other for many minutes. Both were crying, shedding tears and sobbing before Munna Bai separated them. Munna Bai had also become emotional and with teary eyes, she patted both mother and daughter to comfort them.

Munna Bai asked Jyoti to take her mother to her room and help her to freshen up and then come out for lunch.

After about forty five minutes, Roselyn, Jyoti and Munna Bai were taking lunch together.

While taking lunch, Munna Bai told Jyoti to discuss her future course of action with her mother and that she was free to take any decision whatsoever including going back to Amritsar with her mother.

After lunch, Jyoti took her mother to her room and asked her to take a nap to freshen up as she must be tired by long journey. But Roselyn wanted her to get ready for Amritsar immediately. With lot of difficulty, Jyoti could persuade her to sleep for some time before discussing future course of action as advised by Munna Bai.

Roselyn slept for about four hours. Thereafter, she freshened up and while taking a cup of tea with Jyoti, she started the topic of Jyoti returning to Amritsar.

Jyoti heard her mother patiently and with complete attention and then spoke.

"Listen Mom. Though I have stayed at this brothel for about nine years but I did not have to sleep with any man. Instead, Munna Bai made arrangements for me to study and complete my graduation and looked after me like her own daughter. Thereafter she has made me head of her business organization", Jyoti explained.

"Do you know that she also arranged to take revenge against JP and Manchanda on my behalf as they had raped me in Amritsar and thereafter traded me like a commodity", Jyoti added.

"Oh my God. Did Munna Bai arrange to attack and injure them so severely to take revenge for your suffering", Roselyn exclaimed.

"Yes Mom", Jyoti replied in a very cold tone.

"I am so grateful to her for looking after my daughter so well. She must be very kind hearted", Roselyn said in an appreciative manner.

"Yes, she is and I cannot leave her and go to Amritsar after she has done so much for me", Jyoti told Roselyn in a very straight forward and determined manner.

Roselyn kept looking at Jyoti for some long moments before telling Jyoti, "But this brothel is not a place for you to spend your life".

"This brothel is like a sacred place for me", Jyoti replied.

Roselyn was stunned and had no immediate reply.

Jyoti was searching something in her drawer. She took out a revolver and showed it to Roselyn.

"This revolver has been gifted to me by Munna Bai. I keep it loaded for my self-defense. It has six bullets", Jyoti told her mother with a smile on her face.

Roselyn wanted to say something but Jyoti stopped her.

"We can discuss it later if you wish. Now you should take rest and sleep. It is night time already", Roselyn said and both mother and daughter started preparing for good night sleep.

Next day, Jyoti got up early and was busy with her drug trade operations while Roselyn woke up late. Roselyn had her breakfast alone at about 11.00AM and looked for Jyoti.

After about an hour, Roselyn joined Jyoti in her office. She heard Jyoti talking to some people on phone and discussing drugs. She was quite surprised and bewildered, not knowing how Jyoti was concerned with drugs.

After Jyoti got free from phone calls, Roselyn asked her, "Jyoti! What is your business? In what context, you were mentioning about drugs?

Jyoti looked at her mother and replied, "My organization deals with drugs of very high quality and many of these are imported. We sell these drugs to very rich and celebrity clients. Our business is spread over Mumbai, Delhi, Chennai and Hyderabad. Our plans are to further expand this business to other parts of India and after some time, we may start exporting them to neighbouring countries too. This business is highly profitable and I am the head of this business".

Roselyn was shocked to see Jyoti talking so casually about her drug trade and boasting about profitability aspects.

"Do you know that drug trading is an illegal trade"? Roselyn asked Jyoti.

"Yes, I know. But we deal in only very superior drugs and with only very rich and celebrity clients. So there is no risk, especially because police do not interfere with rich and celebrity clients", Jyoti replied.

"But, it is illegal and you can be caught any time. Moreover, with drugs, you are destroying lives of people. Drugs are no good for anybody – rich or poor", Roselyn tried to counsel Jyoti.

"Oh no Mom! I have been dealing in drugs since about three years. Before that, Munna Bai was dealing in these drugs. Police has never questioned us. Since our drugs are of very superior quality, these don't harm people, instead these help them to gain energy", Jyoti replied.

Roselyn had no words to further counsel her daughter though she knew that her daughter was involved in an illegal trade and was doing something harmful for humanity. But she did not know how to convince her daughter. She murmured her prayers for the good of her daughter.

Jyoti looked at her mother and smiled. She was enjoying her mother's concern for her.

21st October 2021

This was eighth day for Roselyn since she had arrived in Mumbai. She was feeling very uncomfortable by staying at the brothel.

She knew that Munna Bai was a noble woman but she also knew that brothel can't be a respectable place for women.

"Brothels will always carry a stigma and its inmates will never be respected by our society", Roselyn thought.

Keeping this in view, Roselyn had tried a number of times to counsel and convince Jyoti to leave the brothel and return to Amritsar but did not succeed. She had also spoken to Munna Bai to take her help but she had only one answer.

"Whatever Jyoti decides will be acceptable to me", Munn Bai had said.

1st November 2018

It was 4.00 PM. Both Munna Bai and Jyoti were quite disturbed and gloomy faced. Jyoti was speaking to someone on phone.

"Why did you supply those drugs to students? I had very clearly instructed you that you should restrict supply to only senior faculty members and not to supply to students", Jyoti terminated the call and threw her phone on bed in utter disgust.

"What happened?" Roselyn asked Jyoti and also looked at Munna Bai.

"Two students have died in Delhi by taking overdose of drug supplied by our agent. Two of our agents have also been arrested by the Narcotics Control Bureau. It is a big setback to our drug trade in Delhi", Jyoti replied. She was visibly in distress and worried.

Roselyn did not know how to react and what to say.

At night, Roselyn again started counseling Jyoti against her continuing in drug trade and staying in the brothel.

"Let us leave all this and go back to Amritsar. We will not be rich there but will live with dignity", Roselyn told Jyoti.

Jyoti did not respond.

"What was the root cause for your sufferings in the hands of JP and his associates? Why I had to suffer in Jail for nine years? Do you know?" Roselyn asked while looking at Jyoti.

"It was drugs. Your father had sold you for drugs. Drugs don't give energy, instead they destroy people and their homes and families", Roselyn further said.

"Let us go back to Amritsar. I beg of you Jyoti. Leave drugs and this brothel. These will never give you happiness and dignity", Roselyn pleaded with Jyoti.

"Mom! I don't know anything except my drug trade and this brothel. This is my home, more sacred than anything else. I can't and will not leave them, come what may", Jyoti said in a very stubborn manner, leaving no scope for Roselyn to argue further.

Soon Jyoti slept off. But Roselyn could not sleep for a long time. She was thinking about her daughter. After repeated discussions, Roselyn had concluded that Jyoti will not come back to her. She was deeply involved in drugs and not able to realize its adverse effects on people and society.

"I have suffered the consequences of drugs. Drugs destroyed my family", Roselyn thought.

"Jyoti has already killed two students who were sons of some parents. If not stopped, she will kill many more and will destroy many families. I can't let her indulge in sins", Roselyn was continuing with her thought process.

Roselyn got out of her bed and went to the drawer in which Jyoti had kept the revolver. She took out the revolver. Her hands were trembling.

With revolver in her hand, she looked at Jyoti, her daughter for whose sake she had killed her husband and suffered long years of imprisonment.

Jyoti was sleeping in peace.

"She is so beautiful and young. How could she indulge in drugs and be the cause of death of other people? How can she commit sins?" Roselyn thought.

"Pardon me my darling. But I cannot let you commit sins and to live sinful life", Roselyn murmured.

Roselyn raised her arm, went near her daughter and fired three times at her chest from a close range killing Jyoti instantaneously. This was followed by three more shots and Roselyn fell over Jyoti's dead body. Roselyn had fired the remaining three shots into her own head.

Hearing the sound of firing, Munna Bai and other inmates of the brothel came running to Jyoti's room.

With revolver still in her hand, Roselyn was lying over her daughter. Both were already dead. A family had been consumed by drugs.

****

II

HONOURABLE OPTION

Village: Nahaar, Near Gorakhpur

Nahaar is a small village about 100 kilometers away from Gorakhpur in Uttar Pradesh. There are about five hundred families living in this village. Agriculture is the main profession for the inhabitants of this village. But only about ten percent inhabitants own land while others work as contract labour for these land owners. Since not all get work assignments to work as contract labour, the remaining are compelled to perform menial jobs such as household chores, laundry, to look after animals etc for their day to day survival. As a consequence, vast majority of children in this village remain uneducated or at best complete only primary school education and thereafter, are forced by their household conditions to assist their parents to perform menial jobs.

Casteism is also quite prevalent in this village and as a result, so called lower caste people do not have adequate growth avenues to improve their living standard. As a consequence, poor continue to be poor and dependent upon so called higher caste people who are better off with their resources.

January 1984

Mukesh and Tilak, aged 23 and 21 years respectively, were the only two surviving members in their family. Their parents had passed away about ten years back after suffering prolonged illnesses. They had no close relative in the village upon whom they could depend for their education and other needs of the family. They themselves had to look after their parents and for this purpose, they had started performing menial jobs at an early age to earn for the family. As a consequence, the two brothers could not complete even their primary school education. Their being born in a lower caste family, became another handicap which broke their morale quite at an early age.

One evening, Mukesh had just completed cooking of rice and daal meal when Tilak came to the kitchen after completing ironing of clothes for their village customers. He assisted Mukesh to settle down for eating their dinner.

While eating his dinner, Tilak was unusually quiet and thinking.

Noticing this, Mukesh asked Tilak, "What is the matter Chhotu? You seem to be very serious today. Anything bothering you?" Sometimes Mukesh used to address his younger brother as Chhotu.

"Bhai! I am thinking about our future. I have not experienced any improvement in our living standard since our parents passed away. Shall we continue to live like this and end our life's journey as insignificant and menial entities?" Tilak asked in a philosophical manner.

Mukesh looked at Tilak and smiled.

"Chhotu! You seem to have become a philosopher. Do you have anything specific in your mind? Mukesh asked.

"Bhai! I think that we should leave this village and go to some other place where we can get adequate reward for our hard work and where we can hope to prosper and live reasonably a decent life", Tilak replied.

Hearing this, Mukesh became serious and thoughtful. After few minutes, he asked Tilak, "Where shall we go? Do you have any place in mind?

"Bhai! I have heard about Amritsar in Punjab. It is a quiet city unlike Delhi and Mumbai. There is Golden Temple which runs a langar and feed about one lac people every day. We can go there and search for work. I am sure that in a city which can provide free food to one lac people daily, there will be no dearth of work. God willing, we shall have ample reward for our hard work", Tilak replied.

Mukesh thought for few minutes and then agreed with his younger brother. They decided to wind up in the village and move to Amritsar at the earliest.

March 1984

Mukesh and Tilak arrived in Amritsar by train on 14th March, 1984 with a small suitcase and a cash money of five hundred rupees.

After freshening up, they straight went to Golden Temple and paid their obeisance. Thereafter, they went to the Guru Ka Langar and had their breakfast.

After seeing big crowds both at the Golden Temple and Guru Ka Langar, Mukesh and Tilak were confident that Guru Ki Nagri Amritsar will provide them ample opportunities to prosper.

Thereafter, they came outside and approached an old sardar ji standing nearby, who appeared to be a religious and helpful person.

"Sardar Sahib Ji! We have arrived here today from Uttar Pradesh and do not know anybody. Can you please guide us as to where can we get some work to earn our livelihood? Any work will suit us", Mukesh asked with folded hands.

Sardar Ji looked at them to assess their bonafides and after satisfying himself, asked them to accompany him. He brought the two brothers to his house in his car.

After arriving at the house, Sardar Ji offered them a seat in his drawing room and enquired about their antecedents.

"What work can you do best? He asked Mukesh.

"We can perform household chores, gardening, washing and ironing clothes. People in our village treated us as lower caste folks", Mukesh told with his eyes lowered.

Sardar Ji smiled and told the two brothers that all people are equal and there is nothing called lower or upper castes. Quality of people is determined by their conduct and character. So get rid of all such feelings from your mind.

Sardar Ji was an old Sikh gentleman, named Santokh Singh, about seventy years old and lived with his wife, named Charanjit Kaur. Theirs was a big house in a posh colony, having a medium size garden which was not in good shape due to lack of regular care.

The old couple had two children, one son named Amrik Singh and one daughter named Sharanjit Kaur, both married and settled in United States of America. The old couple lived alone in their house.

He offered Mukesh and Tilak an assignment to look after the house including kitchen and garden. He also advised them to set up a cloth ironing table outside the house to iron clothes for the colony people in their spare time. He also permitted them to live in a servant room near the gate.

Both Mukesh and Tilak were extremely happy at the turn out of things so easily in their favour. All the work assignments were in line with what they had been doing in their village. Besides salary, they were also at liberty to iron clothes for the colony people to earn as much as they could through their hard work. Both decided to work hard, honestly and with dedication to earn prosperity to uplift their living standard.

They started working in the house with immediate effect and within two days thereafter, they also set up two tables outside the house and started approaching colony people for ironing their clothes. For colony people too, this was a very convenient arrangement and soon, Mukesh and Tilak started getting ample workload for ironing of clothes.

Besides salary from their Sikh employer, their earning from ironing work rose quite rapidly and they started saving more than two thousand rupees per month. This was virtually a windfall for them as compared to their earnings in their village. Both brothers became very hopeful about their future in Amritsar and started dreaming about a prosperous life.

April 1987

Mukesh and Tilak had accumulated more than seventy five thousand rupees as savings in their bank account which they had opened in a nearby bank branch with the help of their employer.

One day while they were eating dinner in their room, Tilak looked at his brother and smilingly said, "Bhai! I think it is a very opportune time for you to get married and bring a Bhabhi for me".

Mukesh looked at Tilak and thought for some time and then responded, "You are right Tilak. But for you too, it is right time to get married. So we both will get married simultaneously".

Mukesh had sounded very decisive leaving no scope for Tilak to offer a different opinion. Tilak kept silent which meant agreement with his brother.

Santokh Singh and his wife were very happy when they learnt about the decision made by Mukesh and Tilak regarding their marriage. They had started liking the two brothers because of their honesty, good conduct and dedication towards their work. They offered one more room to the two brothers so that they could stay separately with their wives after marriage.

It was also decided that after marriage, Mukesh and Tilak will concentrate on expanding their ironing work by inviting customers from neighbouring colonies too and their wives will take care of household and gardening work. Mukesh and Tilak will help their wives to take care of the garden work till they could do it independently.

October 1987

On 15th October, 1987, Mukesh and Tilak got married to Sarla and Shanti, who also happened to be sisters. Sarla and Shanti were the daughters of a migrant couple from Uttar Pradesh. They both had studied up to tenth standard and were of amicable nature and well versed in household work.

Soon, both Sarla and Shanti took charge of their households as well as their employer's household as per plans drawn by Mukesh and Tilak. Both the young couples settled down well and lived happily as a single family.

Mukesh and Tilak had also started to work on their plan to expand their ironing work by approaching households in neighbouring colonies. Soon, they got encouraging response and as a result, their earnings also increased significantly. Sarla and Shanti also helped and supported efforts of their husbands to the extent they had spare time.

September 1989

Mukesh and Sarla became parents to a healthy daughter whom they named Archana. Both the brothers and their wives were happy with the addition of one more member in their family.

Santokh Singh and his wife too were very happy. They had experienced a small baby in the premises of their house after many years.

With little baby in the family, Sarla could not devote as much time to household work assignments but Shanti willingly and happily compensated by her extra efforts. Sarla and Shanti were a great example of two loving sisters.

While Archana was learning to walk and talk, Shanti also became pregnant and gave birth to a baby boy in August 1991. Mukesh and Tilak with the consent of their wives, decided to make the boy a Sikh.

They approached Santokh Singh and his wife to seek their blessings and guidance. The old couple was extremely happy to learn about their decision and advised them to name the boy as Gurpreet Singh which they did happily.

Santokh Singh and his wife used to spend a lot of time with Archana and Gurpreet Singh which relieved Sarla and Shanti to do the household chores. Mukesh and Tilak concentrated with devotion on their ironing work which was fetching good income to them.

July 1994

Saint Bhavan was a reputed senior secondary school near the place where Mukesh and Tilak lived. Mukesh and Sarla admitted Archana Saint Bhavan school. The school management waived off the school fees for Archana because of her belonging to scheduled caste. Santokh Singh, by virtue of his good reputation, also greatly helped to persuade the school management to waive off school fees for Archana.

Soon, Archana proved herself to be an intelligent student and became popular with her teachers in the school. She seemed to have a natural flare for studies and also took a very active part in extracurricular activities in the school.

July 1996

While Archana was promoted to third standard, Tilak and Shanti also admitted Gurpreet Singh in Saint Bhavan School. This time too, the school management waived off school fees for Gurpreet Singh. Tilak and Shanti did not have to make much efforts to obtain fees waival as excellent school performance by Archana had proved to be a big recommendation.

Having admitted their children in school, Mukesh, Tilak, Sarla and Shanti were sincerely focused on their respective work assignments. They were also serving Santokh Singh and his wife loyally and faithfully like their own children, and the old couple too treated them as their children.

Amrik Singh and Sharanjit Kaur during their visits to India, had also liked and appreciated Mukesh and Tilak and their wives for their services to their parents. They had encouraged them to facilitate higher education for their children and for this purpose, they had assured them all possible help.

January 1998

On 29th January, 1998, Santokh Singh left this world for his heavenly abode after a brief illness. Charanjit Kaur could not withstand the impact of death of her husband for too long and she too passed away on 20th April, 1998.

Amrik Singh and Sharanjit Kaur along with their families came to India on both occasions to arrange last rites of their parents.

While leaving India, Amrik Singh asked Mukesh and Tilak to continue staying in the house and to look after it. He also assured them for all possible help for education and settlement of their children.

January 2002

Both Archana and Gurpreet were doing very well in their academics, but Archana was doing exceedingly well. While she was continuously securing first position in her school, she was also taking part in inter school debate competitions and securing first position for her school. "Casteless society", "Equal Opportunities for Girls" were her pet subjects which she debated very well during declamation contests and impressed the audience with her impeccable arguments.

July 2006

Archana passed her 12th standard examination conducted by Central Board of Secondary Education by securing very high grades. While she stood first in Amritsar district, she secured second position in North Zone. She was also awarded a scholarship for her college education.

She had decided to compete in Indian Administrative and Allied Services examination after her post-graduation and to become an officer in Indian Police Services (IPS). She viewed IPS as a tool to serve poor and downtrodden by providing them justice and protection against exploitation. For this purpose, she opted for art subjects in her graduation studies in college. While continuing to excel in her academics, her debating skills also kept improving and during her final year of bachelors, she was already an acknowledged public speaker, having won many prizes and trophies for her college.

Archana was a rare mixture of good brains and beautiful figure. She was a tall and beautiful young lady, fair complexion and having great sensuous appeal. Many of her male class fellows were attracted towards her but she was single minded in pursuing her studies and had a strong desire to fulfill her dream of joining Indian Police Service.

July 2009

Archana passed her graduation examination and this time too, she topped in her college and secured second position in university.

Thereafter, she joined post-graduation course and completed the same in June 2011. She topped in the university and secured a scholarship for studying PhD but she preferred to compete in Indian Administrative and Allied Services examination to fulfill her dream of joining Indian Police Services. She started in all earnest to prepare for the examination.

September 2012

Archana secured 27th position in All India merit for Indian Administrative and Allied Services. Though she had qualified for Indian Administrative Services but she preferred and opted to join Indian Police Service as probationary IPS officer.

Gurpreet Singh also passed his post-graduation with good grades but he had planned to join banking services.

Archana was invited and felicitated by both her school management as well as college management. Mukesh, Sarla, Tilak, Shanti and Gurpreet were also present on the occasion of felicitation functions. They were all proud of achievements made by Archana.

Archana reported for initial training at Lal Bahadur Shastri National Academy for

Administration Mussoorie. Thereafter she underwent training at Sardar Vallabh Bhai Patel National Police Academy, Hyderabad and at various field positions before her regular posting.

October 2014

After her successful completion of training, Archana was posted in Delhi as Assistant Commissioner of Police (ACP). While she reported to Commissioner of Police, her immediate superior officer was a young IPS officer, named Bhoop Singh, hailing from Jat community in Haryana state and working as Deputy Commissioner of Police.

Bhoop Singh was a tall young man, having good physique and of impressive personality. He was soft spoken and of amicable nature but strict in his police working. He had earned good reputation for himself and his department during his short stint in Delhi by solving few intricate cases involving some famous political names of India's Capital. Despite pressure from senior political circles, he had not yielded ground and in the end he had succeeded in sending the guilty to jail.

Bhoop Singh was senior to Archana by five years. He was quite impressed by Archana's academic records and her keenness to join the Police department in spite of her qualifying for Indian Administrative Services. He advised Archana to work fearlessly and assured her of his full support for actions to make the Capital a crime free city.

Archana was a fast learner. She learnt the intricacies of police working from Bhoop Singh quite fast and soon she started taking on the Capital's goons independently with full support of Bhoop Singh. She also participated in police actions led by Bhoop Singh against renowned criminals.

During these police actions, Archana and Bhoop Singh had opportunities to know about each other including family backgrounds, personal likes and dislikes, ambitions and plans for future.

Archana found Bhoop Singh a soft and sensitive person though he was very strong and strict in his police working. Similarly Bhoop Singh also found Archana a very ambitious young woman, highly dedicated to fulfill her police duties to protect and to provide justice to poor and downtrodden people against atrocities by the resourceful people. He was highly impressed both by her beauty and her dedication to her police duties.

Both Bhoop Singh and Archana were also committed to their families and did not want to do anything which may cause them any disappointment or frustration by their actions.

September 2015

Archana and Bhoop Singh had been working together since about a year and had developed mutual appreciation and respect for each other.

Archana wished to spend her life in the company of Bhoop Singh but was shy to make any suggestion to him in this regard.

It was 16th September 2015. Bhoop Singh and Archana were returning from a police action and on the way stopped at a restaurant and ordered some snacks.

While they were waiting for snacks, Bhoop Singh looked at Archana and straightway asked," Archana! Will you marry me?"

It was so sudden a development that Archana could not respond for a minute or two. She had become just a statute. Her face had become red with shy feelings. Bhoop Singh kept looking at her and patiently waited for her response.

After Archana gathered herself, she shyly looked at Bhoop Singh and then responded with her head lowered, "Yes".

Bhoop Singh was quite surprised but pleased too with Archana's shyness. He took hold of Archana's hands and said, "I promise to always take care of you and never make you unhappy till my last breath".

It was for the first time ever that Bhoop Singh had touched her. His touch sent a shiver through her body.

Archana looked at Bhoop Singh and just smiled as if she was also assuring him her complete loyalty and support for life.

They ate their snacks in silence. Their relationship had so suddenly undergone a sea change. Only few minutes back, they were colleagues doing their police duties but by now they had decided to bind themselves in a lifelong relationship as husband wife. Both were going through feelings of joy and happiness.

After they finished their snacks, Bhoop Singh dropped Archana at her quarters before proceeding to his own quarters. Bhoop Singh did not want to go away from Archana so soon and instead wanted to stay back with her to spend some more time together. Archana also felt the same way but both felt shy and none of the two could take initiative to ask other to stay back.

Thereafter, the relationship between Bhoop Singh and Archana went through a sea change. They frequently dated each other after office hours. Even in office, they could steal few moments to be romantic with each other. Both were enjoying each other's company. Whenever one was out for police duty, the other felt something amiss and eagerly awaited to be together again.

November 2015

CARON hospital was a very reputed hospital in Delhi, well known for its super specialty functions for treatment of various ailments, especially for transplants of human organs like kidneys, heart, liver etc. The hospital also specialized in pediatrics and maternity treatment. The hospital had its own research center too and carried out experiments and trials on volunteers to develop critical medicines.

The CARON hospital was an approximately 15000 crore rupees medical facility, having about 1000 beds for patients and employed about 1500 doctors, nurses and other staff.

It was a well-known fact that the hospital was patronized by a very senior and influential politician of Delhi.

Since about a year, police department was receiving very disturbing information through its intelligence department about some nefarious activities going on in the hospital. These nefarious activities were criminal in nature and violative of law. But the intelligence officials could not gather concrete evidence to prove existence of these activities. As a consequence, police was not able to initiate any action against the hospital authorities. But the sources, which gave information about the nefarious activities, were very reliable and could not be ignored easily.

One day, the Commissioner of Police (CP) summoned ACP Archana in his office. An intelligence officer, who was already present in CP's office, briefed her about the available reports related to CARON hospital. Thereafter, CP gave detailed instructions to Archana and asked her to get on the job with immediate effect.

Archana's brief was to gather concrete evidence to enable prosecution of the CARON hospital authorities involved in the crime and for this purpose, she was to work only with few reliable junior assistants of her own choice. She was required to function incognito in plain clothes in the guise of an ordinary citizen without any protection and also to keep this assignment as a secret. She was given three months' time to complete the assignment.

The assignment was tough and risky too since a very resourceful mafia was thought to be working for the hospital and the mafia people were very dangerous for anybody coming in their way.

Archana applied for three months leave to the Commissioner of Police which was sanctioned immediately. Five junior assistants selected by

Archana, two females and three males, also followed suit and proceeded on three months leave. She had followed this strategy not to arouse any suspicion whatsoever about her assignment.

Archana left her quarters without informing Bhoop Singh and took a two room apartment in an ordinary locality on rent for herself and her two female juniors which she converted into her office cum residence.

Since the assignment was a top secret, Archana did not confide even in Bhoop Singh. However one day, she called him up and made up a story of her family commitment requiring her to be away for three months. Bhoop Singh offered to help her but she did not agree to take his help and instead told him that she will be able to handle the situation herself.

As per plans drawn by her, she and her five juniors started surveillance of the hospital, paying special attention to pediatrics, maternity, and human organ transplant departments. They closely studied pattern of recipients and donors of human organs as well as the babies and pregnant women coming to the hospital for delivery of babies.

Archana and her team were surprised to notice that:

> While recipients of human organs were rich people, donors were invariably poor and records showed them as close relatives.

> Further that while recipients were kept in hospital for longer duration and looked after well, donors were let go soon.

> While recipients came back to the hospital a number of times for medical checkup and consultations, donors never came back to the hospital.

> The pregnant women coming to the hospital to deliver babies were invariably poor. But their care takers shown in hospital records as their close relatives were rich people.

> Most of the times after delivery and hospital stay, mother and their babies did not go back home together and instead mothers went alone while babies were carried by someone other than the mother.

> While babies delivered in the hospital came back quite often for medical checkup and consultations, but their mothers never came back

After having made these observations, Archana and her team mates started contacting donors and women who delivered babies in the CARON hospital. They were surprised to find that their observations were the realty. In fact, few donors had died too due to medical complications for want of medical care.

Similarly, few women, who had delivered babies through cesarean in the hospital had suffered medical complications later for want of medical care.

After further investigations, Archana came to the following conclusions:

- Vast majority of human organ transplants carried out in the CARON hospital were unauthorized and in violation of law.
- Donors were poor people who were paid money to make them agree to donate their organs.
- Poor women were lured by offers of money to become pregnant by rich men and after delivery, babies were kept with the rich purchasers. These transactions were in violation of law.

- Archana and her team also came to know that even the research centre in the hospital was a façade for unauthorized duplication of existing medicines of other companies.

During investigations by Archana and her team, many of the aggrieved donors and women agreed to record their confession statements and appear as witnesses in a court of law.

Archana had collected enough evidence to enable prosecution of hospital authorities for their illegal and unethical deeds in a court of law. She made a detailed report and submitted to Commissioner of Police on 15th February 2016. Based on this report, senior authorities of the hospital including some doctors and para medical staff were arrested and cases filed against them.

Archana's performance was much appreciated by senior officers of the Police department. Her work was also given a wide coverage in the press and electronic media.

18th February 2016

Bhoop Singh and Archana were sitting in a restaurant for dinner. They were taking soup while waiting for food already ordered by them.

Archana looked at Bhoop Singh and said," Bhoop! I am sorry that I had to make up a story to you and did not tell you about my assignment".

"Oh! You don't have to feel sorry. I am sure that there must be some very strong reasons for that", Bhoop Singh replied.

"Yes, I was under instructions to keep it a secret", Archana replied.

"I can understand. These things happen quite often in our department. So don't carry any remorse in your heart", Bhoop Singh patted her hand to reassure her and smiled.

"One thing I must advise you. Since you have succeeded in nailing so many influential people, you will have to be careful about your personal safety. If at any time you feel threatened, let me know without delay", Bhoop Singh added.

"Sure. I will", Archana replied.

After finishing their dinner, both went to their respective quarters.

28th February 2016

Bhoop Singh and Archana had a luncheon date. While Bhoop Singh was already sitting in the restaurant, Archana came late by about fifteen minutes.

Bhoop Singh noticed some signs of worry on her face.

"Anything serious?" Bhoop Singh enquired after Archana settled in a chair.

"Nothing very serious. I just got a phone call today morning threatening me with dire consequences. I got the call traced by Control Office but it was from a PCO and caller could not be traced. Further, just when I was to leave my house to come here, I got a typed letter given to my orderly by a small child of our locality. The letter contained a threat for me. But I don't think it needs to be taken seriously", Archana said.

"No Archana. I don't agree with you. We should take it very seriously especially in view of the fact that you have come off a very high profile case very recently. Some very prominent people have been hurt by you and these people may want to hurt you anytime", Bhoop Singh replied.

Archana just nodded her head in response.

"I can't rely on one or two orderlies for your safety. I will like you to move in with me in my house. Together we can face these threats in a better way", Bhoop Singh continued.

Archana just smiled and said mockingly, "We are not yet married".

"Does not matter. I have three bedrooms and you can occupy one of them exclusively for yourself", Bhoop Singh replied. He was visibly very serious.

After some discussions, the two decided that Archana will move in with Bhoop Singh since in any case, they will get married soon.

On 29th February, 2016, Archana moved in with Bhoop Singh along with some essential items of her personal needs.

April 2016

Bhoop Singh and Archana were living together since more than a month. Archana had occupied one bedroom but they used kitchen together. In fact, Archana had taken charge of the kitchen to decide menu and to supervise the cook.

They used to eat together their breakfast and dinner while lunch was taken in office according to their work convenience. Bhoop Singh frequently praised the quality and variety of food after Archana had taken charge of the kitchen.

It was 24th April and Sunday. Bhoop Singh and Archana had planned to go to see evening show of a popular movie in a theatre in Connaught place. Bhoop Singh was already ready and waiting for Archana. Shortly she also came out of her room dressed in a pink sari with matching sleeveless blouse. Though she had used a very light make up, but she was looking stunningly beautiful and attractive. Bhoop Singh could not take his eyes off her till Archana smilingly waved her hand before his eyes.

Though Bhoop Singh and Archana were sitting in the theatre but it was Archana alone who was seeing the movie. Bhoop Singh was lost in his own thoughts. He was not able to stop seeing Archana before his closed eyes, dressed in a pink sari and matching sleeveless blouse, looking so fresh and attractive, sensuous and desirable.

When movie came to an end, Bhoop Singh was still lost in his own thoughts till Archana placed her hand on his shoulder and shook him. Archana's hand touch sent a strange feeling through his body and he hurriedly got up from his seat.

"Did you see the movie? I think you were sleeping throughout the movie", Archana looked at Bhoop Singh and asked while returning home in a car.

Bhoop Singh looked back at Archana and stammered, "I was dreaming about you".

Archana blushed and looked at Bhoop Singh in a very romantic way.

Bhoop Singh felt a very strange feeling in his body system and he wished to take Archana in his arms but presence of driver forced him to hold himself back.

After about half an hour drive, they reached home. While Bhoop Singh sat down in the lobby,

Archana went to her room and after about fifteen minutes, came out dressed in a light blue sleeveless night gown. She was looking very beautiful and attractive.

"Bhoop! What will you like to eat?" Archana asked.

"You", Bhoop Singh replied in a very naughty manner.

Archana blushed and her face became crimson red. After few minutes, she repeated her question.

"I truthfully replied to you. Now it is up to you whether to fulfill my wish or to turn me down" Bhoop Singh replied.

"You seem to be very naughty today", Archana said while looking at Bhoop Singh and went inside the kitchen.

After about twenty minutes, she came out with some sandwiches and two mugs of coffee and placed on the dining table.

"Come. Let us eat", Archana asked Bhoop Singh.

Bhoop Singh came over to join Archana at the dining table. He was constantly looking at Archana in a very strange manner. He appeared to be mesmerized by her.

After finishing dinner, Archana collected the plates and put them in the kitchen sink.

"Good night Bhoop", Archana said and was about to go to her room when Bhoop Singh caught hold of her bare arm and pulled her towards him.

"Come to my room. I can't sleep alone", Bhoop Singh whispered and kissed Archana.

This was the first time that Bhoop Singh had taken her in his arms and kissed. Archana felt a strange shiver running through her whole body and experienced a pleasing intoxication. She feebly attempted to free herself from his hold but he further tightened his hold. Thereafter, she also surrendered herself to his desires.

Bhoop Singh guided Archana to his room and thereafter they submitted themselves willingly to each other and made love till both felt exhausted and slept.

It was 11.00 AM next day when Archana woke up. She hurriedly put on her clothes and left for her room. Bhoop Singh was still asleep with his clothes lying on floor haphazardly.

Archana sat on bed in her room and tried to recollect what happened during the night in Bhoop Singh's room. She faintly remembered their bare bodies embracing each other with vigor and excitement and both kissing each other like a mad couple hungry for each other. She could remember their bodies becoming one and how they both enjoyed their first union.

Archana was blushing but also got worried.

"We have done something which is permissible only between husband and wife and we are not married yet", she thought.

"This was unethical and immoral", she continued thinking.

"But we have already decided to get married soon", she also thought and tried to convince herself as if they had committed no wrong.

"What if I get pregnant", a thought came to her mind and she felt very disturbed.

"We shall have to get married soon. I will tell Bhoop as soon as he wakes up", she told herself.

Thereafter, she took bath and got ready for the day.

"How shall I face Bhoop?" she thought and blushed with a shy smile on her face.

She went to the kitchen and made arrangements for lunch.

After about an hour, Bhoop Singh also came out of his room. By that time, Archana had already got lunch laid on the dining table. Both Archana and Bhoop Singh took seats for lunch. Both were feeling very awkward and looking away from each other.

After finishing their lunch, Bhoop Singh told her," Archana! About half an hour back, I received a message from my mother. There is some emergency in the family and they need me urgently. I will have to proceed immediately for my village. I have already informed CP'.

"OK", Archana said and looked at Bhoop Singh as if to say something.

"What is the matter", Bhoop Singh asked. He had sensed that Archana wanted to say something.

"If situation permits, talk to your parents about our early marriage", Archana said with her head lowered.

"I will definitely try. You take care of yourself here", Bhoop Singh said and went to his room. After about half an hour, he left for his village.

Archana felt lonely and sad. She spent rest of the day in her room. She had missed her office but fortunately for her, it was a peaceful day and she could handle routine office matters from her residence.

Memories of last night kept coming back to her. She was blushing and smiling but also concerned about her possible pregnancy.

"What if I become pregnant and Bhoop's parents do not agree for our marriage?" she thought.

This thought made her nervous and worried.

"But why his parents will not agree for our marriage? Am I not a suitable match for their son? I am a class I officer. What more they will want for their son?" Archana kept thinking till she slept off. She had not eaten her dinner.

Bhoop Singh was away to his village for fifteen days. Archana felt lonely and sad in his absence. After their night together in his room, her feelings for him had undergone a sea change. He had become a very important part of her life and she wanted to be with him all the time. It had become very difficult for her to live separately from him.

10th May, 2016

Bhoop Singh returned from his village in the afternoon of 10th May, 2016 when Archana was away to her office.

After freshening up, he was taking evening tea when Archana returned home from office.

"Hey Bhoop! When did you come? I did not know you were coming back today", Archana exclaimed in joy. She was visibly very happy and jubilant on seeing Bhoop Singh in the house.

"How was your trip to your village and I hope everything was good there", Archana said.

Bhoop Singh just smiled faintly in response.

"Anything serious? You do not seem to be happy", Archana enquired while sitting in a chair near him.

"You take your tea and change to freshen up. We can then talk", Bhoop Singh said.

Archana sensed something wrong. She took tea in silence and then went to her room to change and freshen up. Shortly she returned and sat near Bhoop Singh. She was wearing a sleeveless T-shirt and pyjama and looking very attractive.

"What is the matter? You don't seem to be happy", she asked.

"My uncle has been arrested and I was busy all these days in that connection", Bhoop Singh replied.

"Why? On what charges?" Archana asked.

"Murder", Bhoop Singh replied. He appeared to be quite depressed and dejected.

Archana was stunned. She was quiet for some time before she asked, "Whose murder? Please tell me everything".

"Archana! We are a joint family. My uncle and father along with their families live together. The eldest son of my uncle, who is a lawyer, fell in love with another lawyer girl and wanted to marry her. He told this to his parents but my uncle did not agree. So the two married in a court. My uncle hired some men and together they murdered the lawyer girl and injured her parents and brothers", Bhoop Singh explained.

"Oh my God!", Archana whispered.

"But what was the hurdle in marriage? Why your uncle did not agree for the marriage", Archana asked.

"The girl belonged to a lower caste. We are Jats which is considered to be a superior caste and highly respectable community in our village", Bhoop Singh explained.

"But this is stupid thinking. The girl was a lawyer, well-educated and a professional like their son. Why should they have objected?" Archana sounded quite angry.

"I agree but this is how it is in our family", Bhoop Singh said in a quite dejected tone.

Archana appeared to be worried.

"Did you talk to your parents about our marriage?" Archana enquired.

"I did not get any opportunity to talk about it", Bhoop Singh replied.

Archana appeared quite tense.

"Bhoop! I too don't belong to a high caste or community. I am from Dhobi caste which is one of the scheduled castes", Archana told him.

Bhoop Singh appeared to be quite disturbed for some moments but he quickly recovered and became normal.

"I am sure that I will be able to prevail upon my family for our marriage", he told Archana and smiled.

"But you will have to act quickly. We were without any protection the other day", Archana said. Her face had become crimson red while saying so.

Bhoop Singh looked at her and smiled.

"Don't worry", he told Archana.

Thereafter, Archana made arrangements for the dinner. After dinner was ready, Bhoop Singh and Archana sat down for the dinner and ate together.

While Archana was happy to have Bhoop Singh back with her, Bhoop Singh was finding it difficult to take his eyes off her. To him, she was looking very attractive and sexy in T-shirt and pyjama.

After dinner, suddenly he got up and went to Archana. He took her in his arms and kissed hard. Thereafter, he started guiding her to his room.

"Leave me Bhoop. Let us not repeat it. It is risky. We don't have any protection", Archana tried to free herself from Bhoop Singh's hold.

"Don't worry. I have brought protection", he showed a packet to her.

"Oh you naughty. All planned in advance", she mocked at him.

"I am now an addict to you. Can't live without you", he said and kissed her again.

She was no longer herself and willingly followed Bhoop Singh to his room.

Once again, they went through fierce love making till they were exhausted and slept off. This time, Archana was also equally active during their love making.

5th June, 2016

It was Sunday. Both Bhoop Singh and Archana were home and had just finished their breakfast.

"Bhoop! I am pregnant", Archana told Bhoop Singh.

"But we have been using protection", Bhoop Singh said. He was visibly disturbed.

"First time, we were without protection", Archana replied.

"Oh", Bhoop Singh said.

"What do you suggest?" he looked at Archana and asked.

"We should get married immediately without any delay", Archana replied.

"Will you like to abort so that we can get some more time?" he asked.

"No. Don't even think of it. We love each other. It is not merely sex", Archana said tersely.

"OK. I will talk to my parents", he said.

"Any undue delay will complicate matters", Archana said.

Bhoop Singh nodded his head in agreement.

July 6, 2016

Both Bhoop Singh and Archana left together for office in the morning. Archana came back home late in the evening. She did not find Bhoop Singh and instead, there was a handwritten note left by him for her.

Bhoop Singh had left for his village as urgently summoned by his parents. He had hoped to return within few days.

Archana was quite surprised. Bhoop Singh had not mentioned anything in the morning or in office to her about his going to his parents.

"It must be a sudden development", Archana thought.

"The visit will also give him an opportunity to talk to his parents about our marriage", she thought and felt happiness in her mind. She smiled to herself and got busy with her routine.

Next day in office, she came to know that Bhoop Singh had taken one month leave for his personal work.

"What could be the matter? Is it the court case against his uncle or some issue related to our marriage?" Archana thought but could not arrive at any definite conclusion.

August 7, 2016

It was Sunday afternoon. Archana was at home and had just finished her lunch when Bhoop Singh walked in the house.

Archana was happy and excited the moment she saw him and went to him with a broad smile on her face.

"Hi Bhoop! How are you? I was concerned and worried for the way you left without even telling me. Is everything fine in your family in the village?" Archana said everything in one breath.

Bhoop Singh smiled at her anxiety and questions. He signalled her to sit down. Thereafter he went to his room and came out after few minutes.

"So how are you Archana? I hope everything was fine here in my absence", he asked Archana.

"Yes except that I missed you so much. I was also concerned and worried for you and your family and the way you left without even telling me", Archana replied with a trace of complaint in her voice.

"I am sorry. The message from my father was so urgent that I missed to even inform you while leaving for my village", he explained.

"OK. Now since you are here with me, let us leave this topic and tell me about your latest", she said.

"I have married", he just blurted out.

"Bhoop! Just don't joke. How can you marry without me being there with you? Just tell me about your latest" she asked Bhoop Singh.

"Honestly Archana. I have married. The girl is a doctor practicing in Chandigarh and she belongs to a Jat family of our village", Bhoop Singh replied.

Seeing his serious face, Archana also became serious and tense.

"But how could you do it? What about our relationship?" she asked him. She was angry and disbelieving.

"Look Archana. I tried to persuade my parents but my father was not ready to accept my marriage with a girl of low caste community, irrespective of her high rank and status in society. And you know what had happened in the case of my uncle's son. I did not want similar fate for you and your family. To protect you, I had to agree to marry the girl of their choice", Bhoop Singh explained.

"This way, I protected you and your family as well as my own family. This was the best way to go about", he further added.

"What about me and our baby which is already there within me", she enquired.

"Abortion, as also earlier suggested by me, is the easiest way out. Thereafter, you can also move forward in life by marrying some suitable match which will not be difficult for you to find", Bhoop Singh replied.

"Bhoop Singh! You did not protect anyone, neither me, nor my family or your family. You are simply a coward. You don't have courage to stand up for your promises and commitment. It was my mistake that I could not judge you correctly and fell for you", Archana spoke angrily.

"It is your view. But I did what I thought to be the best option", Bhoop Singh said as a matter of fact.

Archana heard this with her face red with anger.

She angrily went to her room and soon came out with her service revolver in her hand.

She aimed the revolver at Bhoop Singh and said angrily," Bhoop Singh! I am ashamed that I loved a person like you. You will never be a husband, father or a son to be proud of. You don't even deserve to live anymore", and then fired and emptied the revolver killing him on the spot.

Half an hour later, Archana was at the residence of Commissioner of Police to surrender herself.

She had informed the Commissioner that she had shot and killed Bhoop Singh, her senior.

"Why did you kill him?" the Commissioner had asked her.

"Sir! That was the only Honourable Option available to me", she had replied.

III

WARRIORS

Though I was born in Jammu (J&K), but was brought up in Amritsar (Punjab) since I was a few months old baby. Amritsar is an international border city famous for its religious, pilgrimage and historical importance. Natives of Amritsar are exceptionally hospitable, ever ready to entertain even strangers with open arms. Golden Temple, which is the Supreme Center of Sikhism and most sacred for Sikhs and Punjabis in general, is also situated here.

I always had great fascination for Amritsar, and did not want to live any time far from it. But destiny took me away to various parts of India and I could return to Amritsar only after more than three decades when I retired from my railway service in 2005.

I was happy to be back in Amritsar and quickly settled down along with my wife – children being away to their work places.

With great enthusiasm, I started re-exploring Punjab in general and Amritsar in particular, by interacting with people wherever I could meet them as well as through newspapers and magazines.

Soon I could sense that Amritsar and Punjab were no longer the same as in my old times. Though, entire India had undergone a change over the years but deterioration in Punjab and Amritsar was much more pronounced. Corruption had taken deep roots in government departments and it was almost impossible to get a government job, big or small, done without greasing palms of the powerful. No one seemed to be working to rout out corruption from the system and that saddened me a lot.

It was 8th September, 2006 and I was quite sad and feeling pessimist. I did not know how I could help to cleanse the government system in Punjab. I kept thinking and my mind was working overtime but I had no solution. This state of my mind continued even on 9th September till I retired for the good night sleep.

Did I have a good night sleep?

Fact was that I did not sleep at all. Instead, it seemed that I was hypnotized for long hours and made to watch a movie playing before my eyes. The movie played as below:

****

September XXXA, Chandigarh

It was Monday, the 11th September. About twenty young boys and ladies, all in their mid-twenties, were sitting in a big room of a government building. The room was neat and clean, air-conditioned and well furnished.

These young boys and ladies had been selected on basis of their performance in written examination and called for interview for gazetted posts in Punjab State Civil Services. The interview was scheduled to commence at 10.00 AM.

At 11.15 AM, an office staff came there and announced that interview had been rescheduled to commence after lunch break at 2.30 PM due to one member of the interview board not turning up because of his urgent engagement.

All but four of the candidates left the room and went out. The left over four candidates stayed back since they had come from outstation and had no place to go. It was also their first visit to Chandigarh and they were not familiar with the geography of the city.

Soon, they started conversation among themselves and developed a common subject for their discussions. They were very critical of widespread corruption prevailing in Punjab and wished to join State Civil Services to cleanse it from within by becoming a part of it.

Their names were Ranjit Sharma, Harjeet Singh, Kulbhushan Gupta and Surinder Singh Bhatia. They belonged to Amritsar, Tarn Taran, Ludhiana and Gurdaspur respectively in Punjab.

While Ranjit Sharma and Harjeet Singh had passed MBBS and B.Tech respectively, Kulbhushan Gupta and Surinder Bhatia had passed MSc. One thing common in them was that they all were toppers of their respective colleges and had obtained very high merit in their respective universities.

Such meritorious candidates in normal course should have been bubbling with very high self-confidence for their final selection but strangely, all four were quite doubtful about their selection for the State Civil Services.

While conversing with each other, they came to know about one more commonality among them.

All the four had been approached and sounded through some intermediaries that they can get selected for the State Civil Services if they can arrange to pay twenty five to thirty lac rupees. Since they belonged to lower middle class families, they could not afford to arrange so much money.

With so many commonalities among them, they soon became friends, having similar thinking about the social ills and administrative weaknesses prevailing in the system and remedies to overcome them. They decided to remain in touch with each other even after the interview and for this purpose, they exchanged their contact details including addresses.

The interview commenced at 3.30 PM and after the interview, all candidates dispersed. Ranjit, Harjeet, Kulbhushan and Surinder bid good byes to each other and dispersed with a reiteration of their promise to remain in touch with each other.

January XXXB

On 22nd January, the result of the Punjab State Civil Services selection was declared. None of four friends, Ranjit Sharma, Harjeet Singh,

Kulbhushan Gupta and Surinder Singh Bhatia was selected. Only Surinder Singh Bhatia could find place at serial number 11 in the waiting list but he never got a call for appointment.

The four friends again appeared in the Punjab State Civil Services in the year XXXB, got selected in written examination and called for interview. This time the intermediaries had raised the demand money to forty lacs and as a result, they did not find a place in the final selection list.

In the meantime, Ranjit and Harjeet had found employment in a private hospital and a factory respectively at much lower salaries than those paid to the State Civil Services officers. Kulbhushan and Surinder were employed in private offices at quite low salaries which were not enough even to take care of a small family. All the four friends, though intelligent and capable, were employed in positions much lower than they thought to have deserved. This had caused a great deal of dissatisfaction and frustration to them and they were not able to work even in their present positions with complete dedication and capability.

They could not ignore the fact that they were not selected for State Civil Services just because they could not pay huge demand money.

April XXXC

It was 13th April. Ranjit, Kulbhushan and Surinder got a surprise call from Harjeet Singh. He had invited them for a meeting on 20th April at Amritsar. He did not disclose the purpose of the meeting.

When enquired, he simply said," It is a secret. You will come to know when we meet".

20th April XXXC, Amritsar

Ranjit, Kulbhushan and Surinder arrived at the address given by Harjeet Singh. It was a small house and he was already there waiting for them. Along with him, there was another gentleman, a Sikh, aged about 40 years.

"Meet Mr. Kartar Singh Bedi, Ex IPS officer, resigned about two months back from Police department while working as Deputy Inspector General", Harjeet introduced the gentleman. He also introduced his three friends to Mr. Kartar Singh Bedi.

"Mr. Bedi! Why did you resign from such an important department?" Surinder asked while looking at him and Harjeet Singh.

Kartar Singh just smiled and kept quiet.

"He could not cope up with the corruption and nepotism prevailing in Police department", Harjeet Singh replied on behalf of Kartar Singh. There was quite a bitterness in his voice.

Everybody kept silent for few minutes before Kartar Singh addressed them, "Friends! Call me Kartar or Kartar Singh and treat me as one of you irrespective of our age difference".

Then he looked at Harjeet Singh and said," Let us not be bitter. Instead we should find a way to contribute positively to improve the situation".

Thereafter, Harjeet started addressing his three friends while Kartar Singh also listened attentively.

"Friends! Just recall our first meeting at Chandigarh where we had gone for interview with a hope for selection to join State Civil Services. We wished to serve our State and people with honesty and dedication. We also wished to eliminate corruption from our system by joining it. But we were not selected because we could not pay huge amount of bribe. We attempted again but failed for similar reason. We are intelligent, dedicated, honest and competent but not fit for selection because we cannot pay bribe money to the concerned authorities".

Harjeet Singh paused, took a sip of water and continued addressing," Friends! About a month back, I came in contact with Shri Kartar Singh Bedi, who has been an IPS officer for about fifteen years. He has been an honest and dedicated Police officer, helpful to the poor and rich alike, without any consideration of caste, creed and religion. But since about five years, he had been experiencing lot of political interference as well as interference from his colleagues and seniors and behind this all, corruption was the main factor. As a result, it was no longer possible for him to serve with honesty and impartiality. The choices before him were to either compromise his conscious and earn lot of money or quit. He preferred to quit and today, he is with us – without job".

Harjeet paused and looked at his friends. There was complete silence and all three friends were looking at Kartar Singh and Harjeet Singh. They seemed to have lot of questions but none of them spoke anything.

Harjeet Singh started speaking again," Friends! You may be wondering and eager to ask me why I have invited you here."

Ranjit, Kulbhushan and Surinder nodded their heads in unison.

Harjeet continued," Friends! At Chandigarh, I had noticed that all of you and me were eager to work with dedication and follow the path of honesty, and also were determined to eliminate corruption from our system. But the authorities did not give us the opportunity. Even Mr. Kartar Singh, who got the opportunity to join the system, could not continue in the system with his principles of honesty and impartiality and had to quit. I can realistically conclude that at present, there is no place for honest people in our system. Under these circumstances, we cannot hope to see our system cleansed even for next hundred years".

"What can we do?" Ranjit asked. He sounded quite depressed and pessimist.

"Our senior friend Kartar Singh has a plan. But we can proceed to implement it and cleanse the system only if young people like you and me decide to join hands and actively support the plan", Harjeet Singh replied.

"What is the plan?" Kulbhushan asked. He sounded quite enthused.

"Our friend Kartar Singh will explain", Harjeet Singh replied and looked at Kartar Singh.

Kartar Singh stoop up at his seat and started addressing the four young men.

"Friends! First of all I will like to know whether you are ready to struggle and work hard to free our society from corruption and injustice. While fighting for this noble cause, you may not get any reward for yourself and instead you may have to suffer or even sacrifice your life", Kartar Singh looked at all the four young men present in the room with questioning eyes.

There was complete silence for a minute or so before a hand rose.

"Yes", Ranjit spoke in excited voice with his hand still in raised position.

Soon, Kulbhushan, Surinder and Harjeet also raised their hands and spoke "Yes" in unison.

Kartar Singh smiled. He was visibly pleased with the response from these four young and intelligent men.

"Thank you friends", he said and then started speaking again.

"Friends! It is a well-known fact that a criminal will be deterred from committing a crime only if he has a fear of being caught and punished. We have to have a system in which no criminal can go scot free after committing a crime", he paused and looked at the four young men.

Then he continued," Today, criminals are not afraid of law because they are confident of not being caught and therefore there being no punishment for their crimes. Even if caught in a rare case, they can buy the law enforcement agencies and sometimes even the law and go scot free. As a consequence, corruption and injustice is rampant in our government system and society. On record is the statement of our own Prime Minister that when government spends one rupee, only sixteen paisa reaches the ground".

Kartar Singh continued after a brief pause, "Nobody is afraid of law. "Greasing palms to get work done" is the routine. Honesty is laughed at and mocked. Incompetent and dishonest people get what they want while competent and honest people are generally left out".

"Do you agree with what I have stated?" Kartar Singh asked the four young men who were listening to him attentively.

"Yes Sir", all four responded.

"Then what is the remedy?" Kartar Singh asked.

"We must elect only the honest political candidates to represent us in State Legislatures and Parliament so that they can provide us an honest government system", Ranjit replied enthusiastically.

"But where are the honest political candidates? How do we ensure victory of such honest political candidates even if we have some? They cannot spend lots of money in elections to hire goons, to buy influential people to muster votes and for many other things which you all know", Kartar Singh said.

"Then what is the remedy?" Surinder enquired.

"We must create a deterrent", Kartar Singh replied with a grim face.

Ranjit, Harjeet, Kulbhushan and Surinder looked at him. Their face expressions were a clear indicator that they had not understood.

"What type of deterrent and how to create it? Who will create it?" Surinder enquired.

"I have a plan and for the success of my plan, I need your participation with one hundred percent conviction and dedication. I will need you and many more like you. The methodology envisaged in the plan is not legal. We shall have to wage a sort of war against the corrupt people to establish an honest system. We shall have to use some light weapons too to teach lesson to the well-known corrupt to bring some sanity in the system", Kartar Singh paused and looked at the four young men who had become grim faced with frowns on their foreheads.

"Let me assure you gentlemen. If we let the system keep working as it is, we will not have an honest system even during next hundred years. Rather, the conditions will deteriorate and people's lives will become much more difficult and miserable", Kartar Singh added.

There was silence and none spoke for few long minutes.

"Let us have some time to think and we can meet again after few days. After all it is a big decision to be made", Harjeet Singh suggested.

Kartar Singh agreed and they decided to again meet on 27th April at the same venue.

27th April XXXC, Amritsar

Kartar Singh and the four friends were present. Kartar Singh started the proceedings.

He stood up and asked the four young men, "Friends! What have you decided?"

Harjeet Singh stood up and addressed others," I have thought a lot during last one week. I am of the opinion that someone will have to bell the cat. Why not me? Unless we rectify the system, our future generations will also keep suffering. I am in for the plan despite the risks involved".

Ranjit, Kulbhushan and Surinder also stood up in turns and declared their consent to join the plan.

Kartar Singh was visibly pleased.

He rose from his seat and started addressing them, "Friends! Thank you so much for supporting and joining my plan. I am so pleased today and am confident that we all five together will start a revolution which will help our people and also guide the future generations to live a dignified life free from corruption and injustice. We together shall function as Warriors".

He paused and then started speaking again," Now since we all five are together, let me explain my plan to you".

"For next one year, we shall continue to be a group of five only and will not add any other member. During this one year, we shall implement our plan in a limited way, main objective will be to give a practical shape to the plan. In other words, you may call it a pilot project. Keeping this in view, we shall operate only in Punjab.

Each one of you will personally operate in one of the Punjab districts at a time. In Chandigarh, we shall cover only the Punjab government establishments. After each operation, you will quickly move to other district. This will ensure that you will not be traced and caught by law enforcement agencies.

Further, you four will not interact with each other in person or through telephone for next one year. You will interact with me only and that too only when I contact you. You will contact me only when there is a dire necessity.

We shall together identify the most corrupt persons in each district and kill them one by one. The corrupt persons may include politicians, government officials, businessmen and socially notorious people. Our target will be to kill three most corrupt persons in each district during next one year – i.e. one person every four months in each district.

After killing each person, a computer printed paper will be left near the dead body. The paper will have following message:

"You have been punished for your corrupt behaviour towards people of Punjab State. This is also a warning to other corrupt people of Punjab. They should better improve or otherwise will meet similar fate. We have no political affiliation. Instead we are anti-corrupts.

Warriors"

This will create a panic which in turn will act as a deterrent among corrupt people and hopefully they will not indulge in corrupt behaviour or at least number of corrupt people will reduce significantly. At the end of one year, we shall review our methodology and results obtained and take corrective action to make our methodology more effective as well as to popularize our philosophy in other States too.

"Will public support our violent methods?" Ranjit asked.

"Today, public is tired of wide spread corruption, injustice and nepotism. Democratic and legal remedies have failed to rectify the system. They will welcome any remedy which can rectify the system. Moreover, we don't have plans to perpetuate violence. Instead, we want to create a deterrent only", Kartar Singh replied.

Surinder stood up and asked, "We are not rich people. How shall we have weapons? During the year, we will not have regular jobs. How shall we survive without money?"

Ranjit, Kulbhushan and Harjeet also nodded their heads to support what Surinder had said.

"I have my savings which will last us for about two years. I could save this money since I had not married keeping in view the prevailing conditions in Police department as well as in our society and my inability to compromise my conscious. My younger brother will take care of my old parents", Kartar Singh replied.

For fund requirements beyond two years, I am confident that more warriors will join us and we shall also be able to find ways and means to arrange funds. All depends upon how much we succeed in our endeavor? Kartar Singh said.

"Please remember our freedom fighters like Chander Shekhar Azad, Bhagat Singh, Raj Guru,

Sukhdev and others who fought valiantly against the British. They were also not rich", he added.

"What about weapons and how shall we be trained to use them? Harjeet asked.

"I am familiar with the sources for weapons. These will be simple revolvers and it will be my responsibility to arrange them as well as to train you for their use", Kartar Singh replied.

"When shall we start implementation of our plan? Harjeet asked.

"With immediate effect", Kartar Singh replied.

"Ranjit, Harjeet, Kulbhushan and Surinder will operate in Amritsar, Jalandhar, Ludhiana and Chandigarh (including Mohali) respectively. I will be moving within these four districts and will contact you as and when necessary.

Each one of you will get a sort of monthly stipend which will be just enough for you to live and pay for your personal needs besides logistics. First instalment will be paid today before we disperse.

Weapons and ammunition will be arranged and supplied by me personally to each of you. Please bear in mind that you should not share any detail of our plan with anyone outside the group which may otherwise put the plan and our lives at risk", Kartar Singh added.

"Is any time frame to be followed? Surinder asked.

"Yes. Move to your nominated district and start living there by 31st May XXXC. Start gathering information about the most corrupt person in your district and finalize the name by 15th July XXXC. Follow that person to ascertain his daily routine of movements. Keep a tag on him till the day when you have to kill that person.

The date on which you all four will kill your targets will be decided in August XXXC and communicated to you", Kartar Singh explained.

"Please bear in mind that your target must be a well-known corrupt. There will be many such corrupts but you have to select one whom even ordinary public should think to be corrupt so that your action enjoys wider support among the public. In no case, the targeted corrupt should enjoy any amount of public sympathy", he added.

"Which public areas should be surveyed to identify targets? Kulbhushan asked.

"Good question. Let us fix areas for each district for August XXXC", Kartar Singh said.

"It should be state government functionary in Amritsar, a politician in Chandigarh, a police official in Ludhiana and Excise department official in Jalandhar", he added.

"Any other question or suggestion?" he asked.

No one spoke anything.

"Well gentlemen! We have finalized the plan and all of us know our responsibilities and areas of operation. You are all intelligent and I have no doubt that you will execute your part of the operation with great precision and intelligence, without attracting any attention of the law enforcing agencies and certainly without being caught. You are our very precious assets. I wish you success and all the best", Kartar Singh said.

Thereafter, the meeting was over and everyone dispersed.

17th August, XXXC

On 17th August, all State and National daily newspapers carried bold headlines:

"Killer "Warrior" Group born in Punjab.

Kills four VIPs in one day on 16th August, just one day after Independence Day celebrations.

One senior Police Officer in Ludhiana,

One senior MLA (an ex-Punjab State Minister) in Chandigarh,

One senior Nb-Tehsildar in Amritsar,

One senior Excise & Taxation Officer in Jalandhar.

All these VIPs were shot from close distance and they died on the spot. Medical help was rushed in but did not help.

A similar printed message was found near all the four dead bodies which read as:

"You have been punished for your corrupt behaviour towards people of Punjab State. This is also a warning to other corrupt people of Punjab. They should better improve or otherwise will meet similar fate. We have no

political affiliation. Instead we are anti-corrupts.

Warriors"

It is understood from Police sources that they have neither heard nor known "Warriors" Group earlier in Punjab as well as in other States of India. They are hunting for the killers but they have no clue or lead so far.

It is understood from our sources that the four VIPs killed by the self-proclaimed Warriors were known to have amassed huge amount of wealth disproportionate to their known sources of income. Earlier enquiries by various investigating agencies had failed to find any incriminating evidence of corrupt practices against them. Many people among public are of the opinion that "Warriors" have punished the real corrupt people and that this action will serve as a deterrent for other corrupt people. They are happy with this development but don't want to express themselves openly due to fear of the mighty.

Our correspondent has also spoken to some senior people in higher power corridors. They are not happy with this development. In their opinion, this action is illegal and will not help to eliminate corruption. Only legal and democratic procedures can help to eliminate corruption. These senior officials appeared to be quite perturbed and fearful with this development.

Our correspondent also tried to speak to some senior MLAs and State Government Ministers but they all declined to comment. They however appeared to be quite perturbed with this development. It is understood that Cabinet meeting will take place shortly to take stock of the situation.

In the meanwhile, Police Department has been directed to beef up security for the State Ministers and all MLAs besides Secretaries and other senior functionaries of the State Government. Similar alert has been sounded in all other States and at the Centre".

Television news channels were also relaying non-stop news about Warriors and killing of four VIPs in Punjab.

18th August, XXXC

Punjab Chief Minister convened an emergency meeting of his cabinet ministers to discuss the development created by the Warrior's action and to prepare an action plan to apprehend the killers as well as to prevent repetition of this development.

The State Government directed its Chief Secretary to also seek help from the Central Government agencies to identify and apprehend the Warriors.

The Punjab Government, after cabinet meeting, issued a press release assuring the people of Punjab State that killer warriors will be apprehended soon and given an exemplary punishment. The press release also expressed its opinion that the killer warriors belonged to some terrorists group and also enjoyed support of the enemy neighbour country to create unrest in the country, beginning with Punjab, the border state. The Government also assured the people of the State that none will be permitted to disturb the atmosphere of peace prevailing in the State.

The Chief Minister also convened an all-party meeting in the evening during which the latest development created by Warrior's action was discussed. All political representatives barring one were unanimous in their opinion that Warriors must be identified, apprehended and punished soon before they could create unrest in the State. The lonely dissenter advised the Chief Minister to examine the issue of corruption raised by the Warriors and to take effective steps to eliminate corruption from the government system. But hardly anyone paid attention to the dissenter and everyone agreed with the Government's opinion about the Warriors.

The Punjab Government also decided to soon convene the Legislature Assembly to give an opportunity to the people's representatives to express their opinion over the Warriors development.

1st October, XXXC, Tarn Taran

The meeting of five Warriors was in progress. There were expressions of happiness and victorious feelings on the faces of all the five Warriors.

Kartar Singh was addressing the meeting.

"Congratulations my fellow Warriors. Our first operation has turned out to be a grand success. While the precision and focus of our operation has impressed the general public, unfortunately those in power have refused to take any hint or to learn any lesson. We shall have to continue with repetition of our operation till all those in power are forced to take note of our objective and to take visible action to establish an honest society which will be judicious and impartial to everyone without consideration of caste, creed and religion; in which money will not be the influencing factor and in which merit and justice will be the only deciding factors. Our fight is against corruption and injustice and not against individuals.

Our next operation will be in December, XXXC. Exact date and other details will be communicated to you as was done for the first operation.

Please bear one thing in mind, very clearly and without any doubt. Our targets must be real and well known corrupt people. General public must carry conviction about our intentions and objectives. Any wrong selection will give a handle to the mighty to fail our fight".

"If you have any question, you may please ask", Kartar Singh added.

"We are very clear about our fight and its objectives", Harjeet Singh said. The other three Warriors also nodded their heads in agreement.

"Thank you Warriors. I must mention here that we are on our way to fight for the second freedom for our people. The first freedom was from the British and this one is from corruption and injustice. Without achieving our second freedom, the first freedom alone will not yield results to our people for which thousands of Indians had laid down their lives", Kartar Singh said.

21st December XXXC

On 21st December, XXXC, once again all State and National daily newspapers carried bold headlines:

"Killer "Warrior" Group strikes again in Punjab.

Kills four VIPs in one day on 20th December, just about four months after their first strike on 16th August, XXXC.

One senior Minister of Punjab Government,

One very senior Medical Officer in Amritsar,

One senior MLA of the ruling party in Ludhiana,

One secretary level officer handling revenue department in Chandigarh.

All these VIPs were shot from close distance and died on the spot. Medical help was rushed in but proved to be a futile exercise.

A similar printed message was found near all the four dead bodies which read as:

"You have been punished for your corrupt behaviour towards people of Punjab State. This is also a warning to other corrupt people of Punjab. They should better improve or otherwise will meet similar fate. We have no political affiliation. Instead we are anti-corrupts.

Warriors"

We shall like to remind our readers that four similar killings were carried out by the self-proclaimed Warriors about four months back on 16th August, XXXC. The police is yet to solve the mystery of those killings.

It is understood from Police sources that they have not been able to find any trace of the Warriors so far despite having help from the Central agencies. They are still on the hunt for the Warriors but they have no clue or lead so far.

It is understood from our sources that the four VIPs killed by the self-proclaimed Warriors were known to have amassed huge wealth disproportionate to their known sources of income, like the earlier four killed by the Warriors. Earlier enquiries by various investigating agencies had failed to find any incriminating evidence of corrupt practices against these four killed. Many people among public are of the opinion that Warriors have punished the real corrupt people and that this action will, sooner or later, serve as a deterrent for other corrupt people. They are happy with this development but prefer not to express themselves openly due to fear of the mighty.

Our correspondent has also spoken to some senior people in higher power corridors. They are not happy with this development. In their opinion, this action is illegal and will not help to eliminate corruption. Only legal and democratic procedures can help to eliminate corruption.

Our correspondent also tried to speak to some senior MLAs and State Government Ministers but they all declined to comment. They are however quite unhappy with the Police department for its failure to apprehend the killers.

It is understood that Cabinet meeting will take place shortly to take stock of the situation. In the meanwhile, Police Department has been directed to beef up security for the State Ministers and all MLAs besides Secretaries and other senior functionaries of the State Government all over the State. Similar alert has been sounded in all other States and at the Centre".

Television news channels were also relaying non-stop news about Warriors and killing of four VIPs in Punjab. They had invited comments from people belonging to various sections of the society.

While general public have welcomed the development as a ray of hope to make Indian society free from corruption, most of the political people have branded the Warrior's act as that of Naxalites and Maoists. They are worried that if not checked effectively, there will be no rule of law in India.

Some people have also branded the Warriors as revolutionaries like Chander Shekhar Azad, Bhagat Singh, Raj Guru and Sukhdev with the mission to make India a society free from corruption and injustice and livable with dignity.

22nd December, XXXC

Punjab Chief Minister convened an emergency cabinet meeting to discuss the development created by Warrior's action and to review the progress of its earlier action plan to apprehend the killers as well as to prevent repetition of this development.

The State Government reiterated its earlier instructions to its Chief Secretary and asked him to seek more help from the Central Government agencies to identify and apprehend the Warriors.

The Punjab Government, after the cabinet meeting, issued a press release assuring the people of Punjab State that killer Warriors will be apprehended soon and given an exemplary punishment. The press release also reiterated its earlier opinion that the killer Warriors belonged to some terrorists group and also enjoyed support of the enemy neighbour country to create unrest in the country, beginning with Punjab which is a border State. The Government also assured the people of the State that none will be permitted to disturb the atmosphere of peace prevailing in the State.

The Government also announced a cash award of one crore rupees to anyone helping the Government to apprehend the killer Warriors.

The Chief Minister also convened an all-party meeting in the evening during which the latest development created by Warrior's action was discussed. Like last meeting, all political representatives barring one were unanimous in their opinion that Warriors must be identified, apprehended and if necessary, eliminated soon before they could create unrest in the State. The lonely dissenter reiterated his advice to the Chief Minister to examine the issue of corruption raised by the Warriors and to take effective steps to eliminate corruption from the government system. But like last time, hardly anyone paid any serious attention to the dissenter and everyone agreed with the Government's opinion about the Warriors.

The opposition party, in view of failure of the State Government to apprehend Warriors, demanded imposition of President Rule in the State. To counter this demand, the Punjab Government decided to soon convene the Legislature Assembly to give another opportunity to the people's representatives to express their opinion about the Warriors development as well as to prove its majority in the Legislature Assembly.

31st December, XXXC, Jalandhar

While rich and mighty were busy with their celebrations to bid good bye to XXXC and to welcome New Year XXXD, the five Warriors were holding a meeting to review their last operation carried out on 20th December.

"Dear Warriors! Once gain congratulations and thank you all for the success of our second operation. Now we are to plan for our third operation. Do you have any suggestion to make it more effective and meaningful?" Kartar Singh said while addressing the Warriors.

Ranjit rose and said, "We should plan our third operation on 26th January to achieve maximum publicity and impact".

"My dear Warriors! Let us not forget that our fight is only for elimination of corruption from our government system. 26th January and 15th August are very sacred days in the history of our beloved India and these two days represent sacrifices by hundreds of thousands of Indians over more than a century. We must not do anything to disturb the sanctity of these two sacred days. Instead, we must be prepared to sacrifice even our own lives to preserve and maintain the sanctity of these two sacred days even when we have serious complaints against our rulers", Kartar Singh said. His face radiated firmness and decisiveness.

"I am sorry. I did not think from that perspective", Ranjit replied with folded hands.

Then Kulbhushan rose and said "Our third operation should be exclusively against senior political leaders in power. In my view, they are the real culprits for spread of corruption".

Surinder suggested, "Our letter which we leave near the dead, should list our suggestions and demands".

Harjeet rose and responded," We should refrain from listing our demands as that will tantamount to expressing our wish to administer the system. Instead, we should continue with general letter as in the past".

"Thank you Warriors for your suggestions. Our third operation will be carried out in March, XXXD and details will be communicated to you as in the past", Kartar Singh said.

The meeting was concluded and all the five Warriors dispersed.

21st March XXXD

On 21st March, XXXD, once again all State and National daily newspapers carried bold headlines:

"Killer "Warrior" Group strikes third time in Punjab.

Kills four senior Ministers of Punjab Government in one day on 20th March, one each in Amritsar, Pathankot, Ferozepur and

Bathinda where they had gone to inspect some works pertaining to their ministries.

All these Ministers were shot from close distance and died on the spot. Medical help was rushed in but failed to save them.

A similar printed message was found near all the four dead bodies which read as:

"You have been punished for your corrupt behaviour towards people of Punjab State. This is also a warning to other corrupt people of Punjab. They should better improve or otherwise will meet similar fate. We have no political affiliation. Instead we are anti-corrupts.

Warriors"

We shall like to remind our readers that the self-proclaimed Warriors had killed eight VIPs earlier too, four each on 16th August and 20th December, XXXC.

The police has not been able to solve the mystery of those killings yet.

It is understood from Police sources that they have not been able to find any trace of the Warriors so far despite having help from the Central agencies. They are still on the hunt for the Warriors but they have no clue or lead so far.

It is understood from our sources that the four Ministers killed by the self-proclaimed Warriors were known to have amassed huge wealth disproportionate to their known sources of income, like the earlier VIPs killed by the Warriors. Many people among public are of the opinion that Warriors have punished the real corrupt people and that this action will, sooner or later, serve as a deterrent for other corrupt people. They are happy with this development but prefer not to express themselves openly due to fear of the mighty.

Our correspondent has also spoken to some senior people in higher power corridors. They continue to be unhappy with this development. They persist with their earlier opinion that Warrior's action is illegal and killings will not help to eliminate corruption. Only legal and democratic procedures can help to eliminate corruption.

Our correspondent also tried to speak to some senior MLAs and State Government Ministers but they all declined to comment. They however are quite unhappy with the Police department for its failure to apprehend the killers.

It is understood that Cabinet meeting will take place shortly to take stock of the situation. Thereafter, the State Government will send a detailed report to the Central Home Minister as demanded by the Home Ministry.

The Chief Minister is also understood to have briefly apprised the Prime Minister about the killings.

Central Home Ministry has sent an advisory to all States to alert their police forces to prevent such killings in their respective States".

Television news channels were also relaying non-stop news about Warriors and killing of four Ministers in Punjab. They had invited comments from people belonging to various sections of the society.

While general public had welcomed the development as a ray of hope to make Indian society free from corruption, most of the political people had branded the Warrior's act as that of Naxalites and Maoists. They were worried that if not checked effectively and soon, there will be no rule of law in India.

Some ordinary citizens have equated the Warriors to revolutionaries like Chander Shekhar Azad, Bhagat Singh, Raj Guru and Sukhdev with the mission to make India a society free from corruption and injustice and livable with dignity.

The Punjab Government issued a press release reiterating its assurance to the people of Punjab State that killer Warriors will be apprehended soon and given an exemplary punishment. The press release also reiterated its earlier opinion that the killer Warriors belonged to some terrorists group and also enjoyed support of the enemy neighbour country to create unrest in the country, beginning with Punjab – a border State. The Government also assured the people of the State that none will be permitted to disturb the atmosphere of peace prevailing in the State.

The State Government also increased the cash award to ten crore rupees to anyone helping the Government to apprehend the killer Warriors.

Some TV Channels and newspapers also mentioned in their coverage that while most of the political people and senior officials have condemned the killings, general public have welcomed the killings and hope that this may help to eliminate wide spread corruption and thereby cleanse the system.

31st March, XXXD, Batala

Kartar Singh was addressing the four Warriors in a small room.

"Once again, Dear Warriors! Thank you and congratulations for the perfectly executed operation. I can assure you that our three operations will help a great deal to achieve our objective of freeing our system from corruption to a large extent. While our operations have instilled fear in the minds of corrupt politicians and bureaucrats, these have also drawn the attention of common man towards prevailing corruption and awakened them to demand its elimination".

"How long shall we continue with our operations?" Harjeet asked.

"I hope that soon, some Warriors will be born in other States too. If not, we shall have to ignite fire in other States and ensure that Warrior groups take shape soon there too. Unless Warriors are born all over India, our system cannot be free from corruption and injustice.

We shall remotely monitor the impact of our three operations in Punjab. We shall wait for nine months for our next operation. In the meantime, we shall evaluate the impact of our operations carried out so far. If necessary, we shall encourage more Warriors to join our group so that we can carry out our operations on a larger scale. We shall let our three operations be a warning to the mighty and powerful to improve and ensure a system free from corruption and injustice", Kartar Singh said.

Thereafter, the meeting was concluded.

2nd May, XXXD

On 2nd May, XXXD, all State and National daily newspapers in India carried bold headlines:

"Warrior" Group born in Haryana too. Commences its operations on May Day.

Kills two senior Ministers and three senior bureaucrats of Haryana Government on 1st May, one each in Sonepat, Panipat, Ambala, Chandigarh and Karnal.

All these Ministers and bureaucrats were shot from close range and died on the spot. Medical help was rushed in but failed to save them.

A similar printed message was found near all the five dead bodies which read as:

"You have been punished for your corrupt behaviour towards people of Haryana State. This is also a warning to other corrupt people of Haryana. They should better improve or otherwise will meet similar fate. We have no political affiliation. Instead we are anti-corrupts.

"Haryana Warriors"

We shall like to remind our readers that the self-proclaimed Warriors group in Punjab had killed twelve Ministers, MLAs and senior government officials in their three operations in XXXC and XXXD.

The police is yet to solve the mystery of those killings.

It is understood from Haryana Police sources that they have not been able to find any trace of the Haryana Warriors so far despite having help from the Central and neighbouring State agencies. They are still on the hunt for the Haryana Warriors but they have no clue or lead so far.

It is understood from our sources that the five killed by the self-proclaimed Haryana Warriors were known to have amassed huge wealth disproportionate to their known sources of income. Despite public demand, the State government had failed to investigate the deceased's wealth. Many people among public are of the opinion that Haryana Warriors have punished the real corrupt people and that this action will, sooner or later, serve as a deterrent for other corrupt people. They are happy with this development but prefer not to express themselves openly due to fear of the mighty.

While general public has welcomed the development as a ray of hope to make Indian society free from corruption, most of the political people have branded the Warrior's act as that of terrorists, Naxalites and Maoists. They are worried that if not checked effectively and soon, there will be no rule of law in India".

11th May, XXXD, New Delhi

The Central Cabinet meeting presided over by the Prime Minister (PM) was in progress. The PM expressed his serious concern on the development of Warrior groups in Punjab and Haryana, and also the fact that these Warrior groups have been widely supported by the general public. He stated that his government must take serious and immediate action to eliminate corruption from government system before Warrior groups come up in other States too and lead to chaos and anarchy as well as overthrow of elected governments in States and at the Centre.

After detailed deliberations, following decisions were taken:

A general notification will be issued immediately, asking people including PM, Chief Ministers

(CMs) Ministers of Central and State governments, MPs/MLAs/MLCs, government employees to disclose their illegal wealth and assets within two months and surrender to the treasury. Those who fail to do so and if caught later, will be punished severely including imprisonment and confiscation of their wealth and assets.

After two months of the notification:

i) Enforcement Directorate (ED) will investigate each of the Central Ministers including the PM. All these investigations will be completed within four months. The ED's reports will be submitted to the President of India, PM and also made public.

ii) Special Investigating Teams (SITs) will be set up, one each for each State. These SITs will investigate each State Minister including the CM. They will submit their reports within four months directly to the President of India, PM and the concerned CM for action. In addition, SIT's reports will also be made public.

iii) SITs will be set up to investigate wealth and assets of each sitting as well as living former MLA/MLC/MP, and also up to the Secretary, and

Additional Secretary level officers of the State and Central governments. The investigations will be completed within SIX months and reports will be submitted to the President of India, PM and concerned CM for action. These reports will also be made public.

iv)Enquiries will be held through special vigilance teams for those remaining Central and State government employees about whom there will be public complaints.

v) Laws will be revised within two months to enhance punishments for corruption to double of the existing provisions, for members of SITs, ED, Vigilance teams and other investigating agencies.

Punishments for public representatives on account of corrupt practices will also be doubled and will include confiscation of illegal wealth and assets.

All those Ministers, MPs/MLAs/MLCs who will be found guilty of amassing wealth disproportionate to their known sources of income, will also be barred from contesting any election for life time.

vi) Law will be enacted to ensure that:

a) No one will be PM or CM for more than a total of ten years in his/her life time.

Similarly, no one will be a Minister in a State or at the Centre for more than ten years in his/her life time.

b) A person can be made PM only if he/she has served as CM or a Minister in a State or at the Centre for at least five years.

A person can be made the CM only if he/she has served as a Minister in the State or at the Centre for at least five years.

c) No one will be permitted to be a MLA/MLC/MP for more than a total of twenty years in his/her life time.

vii) Law will be amended to drastically reduce the limits for expenditure by the candidates and their parties during elections. Instead, parties will be permitted to campaign through Electronic Media at the government expense. Role of money during elections will be curbed drastically.

viii) Number of political parties eligible to contest elections will be reduced to three each at the Centre and in each State.

ix) There will never be midterm elections for State assemblies. Instead there will be President's Rule in the State till next elections is due if no State party, alone or in partnership with other party, is able to form the State government or if a State Government loses majority support before completion of its legislated term and no State party, alone or in partnership with other party, is able to form the alternative State government.

All newspapers and TV channels in India gave wide coverage to the decisions taken by the Central government to eliminate corruption. People in general expressed their happiness over these decisions and expressed their gratitude to the Warrior groups.

13th May, XXXD, Amritsar

The Warrior group of Punjab was holding its meeting in a small house. Kartar Singh was addressing the Warriors.

"Dear Warriors! You must have read about the decisions taken by the Central Government to eliminate corruption from government system. I am confident that these decisions will help in a big way to achieve our objective of corruption free

India. Credit for this development goes to your honest and dedicated service as Warriors.

Since we have achieved our objective, our group will stand dissolved hereafter.

I suggest that all of you should apply again for Punjab State Services as you had done earlier and I am confident that this time, selections will be based on merit alone without money playing any role.

Good luck folks. Jai Hind"

All five Warriors came out of the house and were readying to say good byes to each other before leaving for their individual destinations. Their faces radiated happiness and great sense of achievement.

Suddenly then, a burst of bullets hit each of the Warriors, killing them instantaneously on the spot. There were about two hundred policemen led by about a dozen of Police officers surrounding the house and aiming their guns at the Warriors. They had fired and killed the Warriors without even a warning or making any attempt to capture them alive.

I suddenly woke up and felt as if someone had shaken me forcefully. My body was wet with sweat even though ceiling fan was running at full speed and room temperature was below 20 degree Celsius.

What was it? What was I watching? A dream of my hidden wishes or a trailer of times to come? Was the "Warriors" only solution to rout out corruption? I had no clear answer.

IV

DAMINI -

The transgender

During my earlier days in Amritsar, I was a regular morning walker. But many years later during my sun set days, morning walk was no longer my cup of tea. I do not know how, why and when I started going out for a walk at noon time irrespective whether it was severe winter or scorching heat of summer, though city remained same.

It was about noon time on 15th April, 2022, a quite hot day and to protect myself from severe Sun, I was walking on pavement of Mall road adjoining Company Gardens. Long stretch of big trees provided an effective shield and protected me against the Sun. Suddenly I noticed a small crowd of people at a distance, everyone looking in the same direction. Curiosity overtook me and I also quickly joined the crowd and almost immediately noticed a dead body lying on the edge of the pavement, covered with shadow of a big tree.

The dead person appeared to be poorly dressed. His face was mostly hidden but otherwise, he appeared to be in his mid-forties. The dead body was certainly not of a woman, though there was something strange about him.

Someone had already called the police who were expected to arrive at the site of dead body any time. Somebody had also arranged a white sheet and was preparing to cover the dead body.

In the meanwhile, an ordinary looking elderly man came and joined the crowd. He stood near me.

Immediately after looking at the dead body, he murmured, "Oh! She is Damini".

I did not know how much of his murmur was heard by others in the crowd but I could hear him clearly. I looked at him and he too looked at me. After realizing that I have heard him, he started moving away from the crowd. Without knowing the purpose, I also started following him and soon joined him.

"Hey! Stop", I told him.

The elderly man stopped and with signs of worry on his face, said, "Babu Ji, I have not done anything wrong. Why are you coming after me?"

"What do you know about the dead person? Who is Damini?" I asked him.

"It is the dead body of Damini. She was a transgender", he said.

"If you knew her, why didn't you help to hand over the body to her family? You could have at least informed her family", I said in a scolding manner.

"Babu Ji, she had no family. She was living a pathetic life. God should not give such a life even to our worst enemy", he replied. His voice sounded as if he was making a prayer to his God, with anguish and deep pain reflecting in his voice.

"Can you share with me whatever you know about Damini? I asked him.

"Are you from Police?" he enquired reflecting suspicion and fear in his voice.

"No. I am a writer", I replied.

"Oh. Then I am ready to share with you whatever I know about Damini but in the process, I shall miss my day's job", he replied sheepishly.

I immediately gave him two five hundred rupee currency notes. This made him happy and relaxed. We two moved towards a concrete bench located in shadow of a big tree and sat there. There was no one around who could overhear our conversation.

"Sir, my name is Kailash Nath and I knew Damini since her birth", the elderly man said in a grim voice and started telling me what he knew about Damini.

****

Kailash Nath and Keshav Prasad were neighbours in Shakti enclave in Amritsar and good friends too. While Kailash Nath served in a factory, Keshav Prasad was owner of a cloth shop which did a good business for him. Since income was good, Keshav along with his wife Sarita could live life like a middle income group family.

Keshav and Sarita were married in 1972 but could not become parent till 1980 in spite of regular medical consultations and medication. This made them unhappy and sad despite being sound financially. Sarita had also tried all non-medical methods like observing fasts, puja, taweez etc as advised by some sadhus and fakirs recommended by her friends. They did not have any of their close relatives in Amritsar. Keshav also used to fully cooperate with his wife in these efforts but to no avail.

While Keshav and Sarita had given up hopes of a baby of their own and were thinking of adopting one from some orphanage, Sarita became pregnant in January 1980 and gave birth to a healthy baby through normal delivery procedure in a maternity home on 29ᵗʰ October 1980. This was nothing short of a miracle for them and they felt ecstatic.

Like others, Sarita and Keshav were also curious to know the sex of their baby. Doctor and nurse had not announced sex of the baby to them as normally done. When Sarita and Keshav looked at the genitals of their baby, they got confused since the genitals were not clearly defined and they could not determine whether their baby is a boy or a girl. They were seriously worried. They feared something wrong with their baby and were quite upset.

At that moment, nurse came there to examine the baby and to enquire about the wellbeing of Sarita.

"Sister! Can you please tell whether our baby is a boy or a girl? We have not been told anything so far", Sarita asked the nurse.

Nurse did not respond immediately. Instead she continued with her chores for few minutes to weigh and check heartbeats of the baby and then replied, "Madam! I do not know. Only doctor can tell" and thereafter she left.

Nurse's face expressions and response reinforced their apprehensions of there being something wrong with the baby and Keshav decided to approach the doctor immediately to seek clarification about their baby.

Lady Doctor, named Sunita, was alone in her office and busy examining some x-rays when Keshav approached her.

"Doctor! can you please tell us whether our baby is a boy or a girl? Why her genitals are not normal like other babies? Is there anything wrong with our baby?" Keshav asked all these questions in one go.

Doctor looked at Keshav whose face betrayed worry and apprehensions to no end and signalled him to sit in the chair lying near him. After Keshav occupied the chair, she offered him a glass of water to calm him down.

After a couple of minutes, Doctor addressed Keshav, 'Mr. Keshav! At this moment, even I do not know whether your baby is a boy or a girl. For that, I will have to carry out some medical checks like Ultrasound etc which will take about two or three days. At this moment, I can only say that your baby is sexually not normal and therefore not definable. Only after medical checks, I can make some statement about the sex of your baby. Further after study of your baby's behavioral responses during next two or three years, we shall confidently determine whether your baby is a boy or a girl. For the present, your baby is normal and you should ignore all of your apprehensions and instead enjoy the baby like other parents".

Doctor's explanation did not calm him down and instead his inner self was more in turmoil. He had however no other option but to go along the doctor.

He returned to Sarita and told her everything whatever the doctor had told him. Sarita became quite disturbed too. However sensing the condition in which Keshav was, she decided to make him peaceful and said, "Dear, let us not imagine things. There is nothing wrong with our baby. You look at the baby yourself. Do you see anything wrong? Our baby is so lovely and charming. Let us enjoy the baby. Even if there is something wrong with the baby, it must be a minor one and can be rectified by doctors. Medical sciences have made great advancement these days".

Sarita smiled at her husband and then signalled him to pass on the baby from the crib to her which he did obediently. Sarita lovingly looked at the baby and then at her husband who was also looking at the baby's face. The baby was beautiful and sleeping peacefully, looking like a small princess. Both felt happy. The looks of the baby had soothed their ruffled feelings.

3rd November 1980

Keshav and Sarita were sitting in Dr Sunita's chamber. After collecting some reports, Dr Sunita started addressing Keshav and Sarita:

"I have carried out medical tests like Ultrasound etc on your baby and have also consulted some specialist doctors about your baby. We have come to the conclusion that your baby is sexually not normal.

Though genitals of your baby are not determinable, but baby has a uterus and ovaries like female babies. In simple terms, anatomy of your baby indicates that her interior is of a female baby but her genitals are not distinctly developed.

At this stage, I can only say that your baby is a female baby, though with non-distinct genitals. Further, we shall have to watch her, both for her physical development as well as behavioral development. We shall be able to make a reasonably clear opinion about her after about two to three years. Broadly, at present, we can also call her a transgender".

"Doctor! will it be possible to rectify her genitals through medication or surgery to make her a complete and normal female baby?" Sarita asked.

"We cannot hazard any guess or give any opinion at this stage. It will all depend upon how she develops with time and what type of medical options or facilities we have in future. For the time being, treat her as a female baby and enjoy her. We shall deal with her case depending upon the conditions arising with passage of time", Doctor replied.

Sarita and her baby were discharged from the hospital on 9th November, 1980. The discharge certificate indicated the sex of the baby as "Female".

Though Keshav and Sarita were happy to have a baby of their own but apprehensions about the future disturbed them quite frequently.

To overcome the environment of apprehensions and worries in their household, Keshav and Sarita decided to celebrate the birth of their daughter and invite their friends over a party. They also decided to use the party time to formally name their daughter.

On 8th December, 1980, the baby was named as Damini in presence of a gathering of about one hundred friends and their families.

****

Damini was growing like any other child. But every new day used to bring increased apprehension and worry in the minds of Keshav and Sarita. They used to frequently watch face and closely monitor behaviour of their daughter. Till December 1982, they did not notice any change in facial features and behaviour of their daughter. It gave lots of consolation and reassurance to Keshav and Sarita that everything was normal with their daughter and nothing will be wrong even in future.

It was 16th March 1983. While Damini was playing with her two friends in the verandah of the house, Sarita was sitting in the chair nearby and watching the kids. While watching Damini, Sarita suddenly became conscious of her acts which were quite distinct from those of the other two kids. Damini had peculiar way of clapping which did not appear to be normal. Sarita was quite concerned and eagerly waited for her husband to return in the evening.

Keshav returned home at about 8.30 PM and after dinner, sat in a chair in the living room. Sarita, after putting Damini to sleep, came to her husband and sat in a chair nearby.

"Keshav! Today I have noticed Damini clapping in a peculiar way unlike other kids", she told her husband.

"What do you mean by peculiar way of clapping?" Keshav asked her.

"Do you remember Dr Sunita had advised us to watch Damini for any changes in her behavioral acts and facial features? She reminded Keshav.

"Today I noticed that Damini was clapping like kinnars", she added.

"It could be just your imagination", Keshav tried to dismiss Sarita's concern lightly.

"No. I am certain about that", she insisted.

Both went to Damini's bed and looked closely at her face. They felt that Damini's facial features were no longer soft and instead some sharpening and hardness had crept in. Her face was tending to resemble that of a male child when observed closely.

They decided to take Damini to Dr Sunita at the earliest possible.

18th March 1983

Keshav and Sarita took Damini to Dr Sunita's clinic and briefed her about their observations about Damini.

Dr Sunita carried out detailed physical examination of Damini and then also decided to perform ultrasound test next day.

On 21st March, Dr Sunita briefed Keshav and Sarita about her findings. According to Dr Sunita, while uterus and ovaries of Damini's anatomy were developing satisfactorily, her genitals remained non-distinct. Regarding facial features, she was not sure for the present.

She asked Keshav and Sarita to keep monitoring Damini and bring her to the clinic at least once in every six months.

This visit to the clinic did not provide any relief or reassurance to them about the future of their daughter. Instead their worries and apprehensions had increased manifold. Sarita in particular was more worried.

While Damini was growing, her voice was getting heavier and her facial features were taking resemblance to that of a male child. However these changes were not very pronounced yet. Only Keshav and Sarita were able to notice these changes while members of their friends circle continued to treat her as a female child.

July 1985

Since Damini was nearing five years of age, Keshav and Sarita admitted her in a nearby school in first standard. She was good in learning and had completed her elementary education at home under the tutorship of her mother.

At the time of admission in school, when Sarita declared her as a female child, the principal was a bit surprised but did not say anything after seeing the hospital certificate. Damini was accepted in first standard as a female child. Keshav and Sarita did not anticipate any problem for Damini since the school practiced co-education.

In the classroom, Damini was assigned a seat along with other girls. She also used washroom meant for female children. Since Damini was sharp and intelligent and learnt her lessons without much effort, she soon became a favourite of her teachers. Soon, she was also able to develop close friendship with few girls of her class.

Though Damini also tried to be friends with few boys of her class, but she was not successful. Boys somehow resented her company and made fun of her thick voice and facial features which were a mix of both a male as well as a female child. Girl students were however more accommodating towards her.

October 1988

Damini was in third standard and a bright student of her school. One day when she returned home from her school, her skirt was wet. On enquiry by Sarita, she explained that she was finding it difficult to urinate in sitting position like other girl students and instead she finds standing position to be more convenient.

Next day, Sarita took Damini to Dr Sunita as Keshav had some important engagement, and briefed her about the latest condition.

Dr Sunita carefully examined Damini. After completion of her examination, she told Sarita that she had not noticed any abnormal development in Damini which may warrant some immediate medical treatment.

"As far as experiencing difficulty during urinating in sitting position is concerned, it is probably due to the fact that her genitals have grown more to be like that of a male child. Let her urinate in a position which is more convenient to her", Dr Sunita added.

"Is there no surgical remedy to overcome this problem?" Sarita enquired.

"No. Certainly not at this stage when she is still growing. May be later when she becomes adult and her genitals stop growing further. Even for that stage, proven medical remedy is not available at present but may become available in future by the time Damini attains adulthood. For the present, concentrate on her studies and make her self-reliant", Dr Sunita advised.

January 1994

Damini had grown to be thirteen years old and her voice and facial features resembled more to a male child. As per Dr Sunita, Damini continued to have female anatomy and for the present, nothing could be done to rectify her anomaly or genitals.

Damini had started facing serious problems in school. Both female and male students resented her company due to her boy-like looks though accepted to be a girl in school records. Even teachers found it hard to decide whether to treat Damini like a female or male student. As a consequence, Damini had hardly any close friend despite the fact that she was among the two top students of her class.

Sarita noticed that Damini had not menstruated yet and she had flat chest like boys. This made her worried and concerned for her daughter's future. She felt miserable, being not able to do anything for her daughter. She had started going to temple regularly to offer her prayers but this too did not help her.

Because of continued state of worried mind and mental stress, Sarita had become sick and weak. Keshav took her to some doctors but medicines did not help her. Her condition continued to deteriorate and one day, while Keshav was at his shop and Damini was in school, she fell unconscious and neighbours took her to the hospital. She remained under medical treatment in the hospital for a week and thereafter died on 29th January, 1994.

Untimely death of Sarita was a big setback to Keshav. Life became very tough for him and he found it almost impossible to manage both his business as well as Damini simultaneously. He knew that coming years were very crucial for his daughter and he needed someone, especially a lady who could devote full time to take care of Damini.

Unfortunately for him, he had no close relative who could assist him.

He tried to engage a whole time nurse but did not get anyone to suit his requirements. Finally he engaged a middle aged woman to look after the household as well as Damini during the day time and at night, he himself looked after his daughter.

Two years had passed since Sarita died. Damini was already fifteen years old. There was no improvement in her condition. Instead, her facial features now resembled more like a male person. Facial hair were also growing, albeit slowly and her chest continued to be flat. She had not menstruated.

Keshav regularly took Damini to Dr Sunita for medical examination but even she could not suggest any medical treatment to make Damini a normal girl.

Keshav was finding himself to be helpless and his inner self was constantly filled with fear and apprehensions about future of his daughter.

"What will happen to Damini after I have gone?" he used to think day and night and worry.

Constant worry was taking a heavy toll of his health and he had become a patient of hypertension requiring medicines on regular basis.

On 27th September, 1996, Keshav died while in sleep. He was found to be dead by neighbours who were called in by Damini when Keshav did not wake up till 8.00 AM on 27th September. Doctor was called but in vain. He also declared him dead. Keshav had died due to a deadly stroke some time during the night.

The dead body of Keshav was cremated with the help of few friends and neighbours.

Since there was no relative to look after Damini, the big issue before the neighbours and friends was taking care of Damini.

"Who will look after Damini?" they thought but had no solution.

One old couple in the neighbourhood volunteered to look after Damini for some time with the help of elderly maid in the house till some permanent arrangements could be made.

No one among the neighbours and friends was aware of medical condition of Damini till Keshav and Sarita were alive. But now, almost everyone became aware of her medical condition.

One day, the elderly couple convened a meeting of few prominent neighbours and discussed the condition of Damini. After the elderly couple explained the medical condition of Damini, they jointly decided to hand over the custody of Damini to the group of Kinnars who used to visit their colony to collect neg whenever there was any occasion of marriage or birth of a son in a family.

According to the decision, custody of Damini along with her inheritance was handed over to the chief of the Kinnars group, named Ram Sultan, on 16th October, 1996. Damini cried a lot. She did not want to go away from her house but no one could help her.

✳✳✳✳✳✳✳✳✳✳✳✳✳

At this stage, Kailash Nath seemed to be quite tired and exhausted. His face reflected signs of pain as if while telling the story of Damini, he had actually lived through it.

"Sir, I could not help Keshav and Sarita during their life time and even later, I could not help Damini. I loved her like my daughter but my family conditions did not permit me to keep her with me", he said.

"What happened to Damini later?" I asked.

"Sir, I do not know personally about her except what I had heard from different people", he replied.

"Tell me all that", I said.

He sat quietly for a couple of minutes as if trying to refresh his memories and then started.

"Sir, It was period of 1996 – 2022, I heard that Damini was living through hell ………………

****

1996 – 2022

Ram Sultan, himself a kinnar, was the chief of a group of about fifty kinnars who functioned in small groups in entire Amritsar city. Their function was to collect neg and badhai from various households who were blessed with a son or who performed marriages of their boys.

Ram Sultan was responsible to look after the interests of all kinnars including their living and lodging. He was virtually the father as well as husband of all kinnars in his group. Kinnars on their own had no sexual identity and acted as males and females according to needs of the group. Most unfortunate aspect of these kinnars was that they had never received any medical treatment and were just thrown out and dumped by their biological parents.

Damini was inducted in the group by Ram Sultan. Since she was young, healthy and had brought substantial inheritance, Ram Sultan kept her as his mistress for first year. Her function was only to please the chief by feeding good food and by satisfying his sexual fantasies.

Since kinnars cannot have conventional sex, they indulged in oral and unnatural sex which was not only painful but also injurious to their bodies and minds. Extensive use of sex toys was quite prevalent among kinnars. For kinnars, these oral and unnatural sex activities were just games and time pass to forget their mental pains and agonies gifted to them by God since their birth for no fault of theirs.

Damini was just a young child, unaware of these sexual games and fantasies. She did not know cooking even. She could not please Ram Sultan who in turn treated her with physical violence and forced her in to unnatural sex causing her severe pain and mental agony. Even some of the kinnars in the group sympathized with Damini's plight but had no courage to speak or act against their chief.

Damini suffered a lot for one year in the hands of Ram Sultan and thereafter, she was thrown in to the hands of other kinnars some of whom also treated her mercilessly for six months.

These eighteen months were hell like for Damini, which left permanent scars on her young and nascent mind. During this period, there was no medical treatment and education for her.

Thereafter she was trained to sing and dance and then she started going out with other kinnars to collect neg and badhai from households.

But probably, she had not forgotten the cruelties and tortures inflicted on her by Ram Sultan and some of her group kinnars.

On 28th September, 1998, only about a month before she became adult, she murdered Ram

Sultan by inflicting multiple severe injuries with a sharp and big knife while he was sleeping heavily intoxicated. That was her revenge against Ram Sultan for his cruelties and torture.

Damini was arrested by the police and prosecuted in the court of law. Keeping in view her age, medical and mental condition, court ordered the administration to send her to Women's Reform Home and also to provide her the best medical attention available.

Damini was kept in the Reform Home and given medical attention but her condition did not improve much. She was also diagnosed for suffering from HIV.

During her stay in Reform Home, she had virtually gone insane and acted like a mad person. She also had some other diseases too, for which she was not taking medicines regularly. As a result, her condition did not improve and instead had deteriorated.

****

Kailash Nath stopped for few moments and then started again in a philosophical manner ....

Today, 15th April, 2022 is a hot day. Heat and her diseases probably did justice to her and she has left this world leaving behind her pains and mental agonies. I am sad to see a young lady, whom I took in my hands when she was an infant, leaving this world but I am glad too that she has gone far away from this world which gave her torturous and painful life.

Kailash Nath started crying and sobbing uncontrollably. I placed my hand on his shoulder to console him but not able to cope up with his pain, I left him alone and walked away without saying "thank you" or even the customary good byes. At a distance, ambulance had arrived and was taking away dead body of Damini – The transgender.

****